JANET EVANOVICH

Thanksgiving

HarperTorch
An Imprint of HarperCollinsPublishers

This book was originally published as a Loveswept paperback in 1988, in a slightly altered form, by Bantam Books, a division of Bantam Doubleday Dell Publishing Group, Inc.

❦

HARPERTORCH
An Imprint of HarperCollins*Publishers*
10 East 53rd Street
New York, New York 10022-5299

Copyright © 1988 by Janet Evanovich
Copyright © 2006 by Evanovich, Inc.
Excerpt from *Smitten* © 1990, by Janet Evanovich; © 2006 by Evanovich, Inc.
Author photograph by Deborah Feingold
ISBN-13: 978-0-06-059880-8
ISBN-10: 0-06-059880-8

First HarperTorch paperback printing: November 2006

HarperCollins®, HarperTorch™, and ❦™ are trademarks of HarperCollins Publishers Inc.

Printed in the United States of America

Visit HarperTorch on the World Wide Web at www.harpercollins.com

10 9 8 7 6 5 4 3 2 1

"That was Tilly Coogan," he said. "And this is Tim. One of my very first patients."

"Are you related?"

"Nope."

"Are you . . . um, friends?"

"Nope."

"Why did she give you her baby?"

Pat put the lid on the top of the applesauce and whistled 'Taps.' "I guess she thought I'd take good care of him."

"You? The man who burns his applesauce and neglects his rabbit?"

"Yup. I'm a little disorganized, but I'm lovable."

It was true, Megan had to admit, he was lovable. She could hardly keep from squeezing him. She guessed he must stand about six feet, but he didn't look that tall. He had the wide shoulders, slim hips, and hard-muscled arms of an athlete, yet he didn't look like a jock. He looked average. The casual, sexy, slightly sloppy version of the boy next door, wearing battered sneakers and threadbare jeans and a gray sweatshirt with the sleeves cut short. And he looked great. He could probably wear his cannibalized sweatshirt to a black-tie dinner and pull it off.

Still, she wouldn't trust him with a baby.

Thanksgiving

Chapter 1

Megan Murphy scuffed through a thick layer of autumn leaves in her round-toed, black leather, gold-buckled shoes. Regulation colonial clodhoppers, she thought happily, bending over to pick leaves out of her buckles. Especially stylish with her blue-flowered thermal underwear and thick gray woolen socks. Yup, she was a real eighteenth-century sex goddess. But hey, it was cold out. Besides, what did the average slovenly trollop wear back then? Silk teddies and designer panty hose?

She did a little tap dance in her big black shoes and kicked at the leaves. When she was a child the leaves in her yard had been immediately whisked away. They were packed in leaf bags, sucked into leaf suckers, or pulverized by the mulch maker, but they were never scuffed through or jumped into or simply enjoyed. That was one of the things that had drawn Megan to Colonial Williamsburg. In its effort to recreate the eighteenth century, Williamsburg had slowed to a walking pace. There was time to enjoy leaves. Even Megan Murphy, who had a strong tendency to hurtle through life at warp speed, found tranquility in the back alleys of Williamsburg.

She scuffed past Raleigh Tavern and along Duke of Gloucester Street to the public garden behind the Prentis House. She settled down on her favorite bench and opened the waxed paper bag containing a cup of hot cider and two sugar cookies from the Raleigh Tavern Bake Shop.

It was November, past the season of peak color for the foliage, and only a few hardy leaves remained on the trees. The new wintery image of lacy bare branches pressing against a brilliant azure sky caught Megan's attention as she tilted her head back, hoping for a few rays of warming sun on her face. A beautiful day, she decided, adjusting her mob cap. In fact, it was better than beautiful. It was perfect. A perfectly beautiful day.

A horse-drawn carriage rumbled down Botetourt Street, and the clop, clop, clop of horses' hooves stirred her imagination. Who had sat on this bench two hundred years ago? she wondered. Maybe it was someone just like herself, basking in the sun, gobbling goodies. Some brazen strumpet, she thought. If she were transported in time she would definitely be a brazen strumpet.

She finished her second cookie and drained the last drop of cider from her cup. She brushed the crumbs off her white linen apron and gaped in horror at her ankle-length, royal-blue woolen skirt. A huge, floppy-eared brown rabbit was eating a hole in it.

"Holy Toledo!" she shouted, jumping to her feet and wrenching the skirt away from the rabbit. She held the skirt up for closer examination and made a disgusted sound at the ragged hem. The rabbit looked at her with wide chocolate-brown eyes and twitched its nose.

"You miserable beast," she said. "Just look at this. How am I ever going to explain this? A rabbit ate my dress? Good grief."

She glared at the rabbit and decided it was

3

the fattest one she'd ever seen. Extraordinarily cute, too. Big and fluffy, with soft brown fur and droopy ears. And it was smiling. Yes, she was sure of it. The blasted thing was smiling at her.

She knelt down and stroked its glossy back and soft ears. Two large shoes appeared beside the rabbit, white tennis shoes that had seen better days. The laces were broken and tied in knots, and the left shoe was stitched together with what appeared to be surgical sutures.

"Trying to steal my rabbit, huh?" a voice said from far above her.

Megan looked up. She could have picked him out of a crowd as the rabbit's owner, she thought. He reminded her of the rabbit. He didn't have big, floppy ears, of course. He had nice little ears that lay flat against his head and were begging to be nibbled. And he wasn't fat. He was just right, in faded jeans and a leather jacket with a red wool scarf wrapped around the neck. But he did have the same incredible chocolate eyes, and his hair was brown, just like the rabbit's, and just as strokable. He wasn't handsome. He was . . . cute. Slightly upturned nose and wide, smiling mouth. A few laugh lines fanning from his eyes. Definitely very cute. And very huggable—just like the rabbit.

"Is this really your rabbit?" she asked.

He scooped the animal up and held it in the crook of his arm. "You bet. We're roomies."

Megan pressed her lips together and swept her skirt out for his inspection. "Well, your roomie ate my skirt."

"Are you kidding me? I hope he doesn't get sick." He narrowed his eyes at Megan. "Bad enough you tried to steal him, but feeding him your skirt! You should be ashamed of yourself."

Megan's mouth dropped open. He was joking, right?

He held out his hand. "Patrick Hunter. Nice to meet you, but don't do this again."

Without thinking Megan shook his hand and mumbled, "Megan Murphy. Okay."

She watched in astonishment while he gave her a funny sort of look, a quick appraisal that lingered for an extra moment at her mouth and ended with a boyish, almost embarrassed grin. He turned on his heel and sauntered away, disappearing behind the scuppernong-grape arbor.

Megan shook her head abruptly. Don't do this again? she repeated silently. Had he actually said that to her? Of all the nerve. She didn't care how cute he was—if she ever saw him and his rude rodent again, she'd tell him what for. She smashed the paper bag into the empty cider cup and stomped off to the gunsmith's shop. "Don't do this again," she muttered. Had he been kidding? She wasn't sure.

Patrick Hunter smiled as he opened the gate to his small, fenced-in back yard. Megan Murphy, he mused. He'd never met anyone so perfectly named. She'd looked like an apparition, standing in the autumn leaves in her colonial dress, with all that glorious silky red hair escaping from her white ruffled cap. She was obviously one of the costumed visitors' aides who sat in front of the craft shops and took tickets. She was average height and seemed to be of average build, but there was nothing average about the riot of freckles that marched across her straight little nose and dusted her rosy cheeks. And there was nothing average about her mouth. It was soft and pink and full. He'd almost kissed her!

He threw his head back and laughed at that.

Wouldn't she have been surprised? Wouldn't he! It wasn't in his nature to go around kissing strangers.

He locked the rabbit in its large wire-and-wood hutch and shook his finger at it. "It wasn't nice of you to eat her skirt. Now I'll have to pay for it, and I'm going to take the money out of your carrot allowance."

Twenty-four hours later, Megan was practically flying down Duke of Gloucester Street. Her black shoes skipped over the brick sidewalk, her long skirt showed flashes of white petticoat as she jigged through a pile of leaves, and her thick, wavy red hair tumbled free, swirling around her shoulders. It was five o'clock, and she had just finished work for the weekend. She tilted her face up into the crisp air and wrapped her long black cape tight around herself. This was her favorite time of the year. Crisp apples, nippy mornings, pumpkins and leaves and . . . rabbits.

She stopped in her tracks and watched the big brown rabbit hop down Duke of Gloucester Street and disappear between two buildings. That was no ordinary rabbit, she thought. That was what's-his-name's rabbit, and it was on the loose, looking for clothes to eat.

She followed it into the little garden beside the bakery, becoming more furious with each step. Obviously, Patrick Hunter was an irresponsible pet parent, not caring if his rabbit got lost or run over by an oxcart or starved to death.

"Poor orphan bunny," she said. She hefted the huge rabbit into her arms and grunted. Okay, so chances of its starving to death were slim. There was still the oxcart to worry about.

Martha Greenwald and Betsy Markham, fellow visitors' aides, peeked into the garden and waved at Megan. "I see you've got Dr. Hunter's rabbit," Martha said.

"*Doctor* Hunter?" Megan repeated.

"He's just moved into town. A pediatrician, fresh out of residency and cute as a button."

Megan pressed her lips together. The guy with the ratty sneakers and leather jacket was a pediatrician? He must have gotten his diploma from the Acme School of Medical Make-Believe. The man was clearly loony. "He should take better care of his rabbit."

"Dr. Hunter's a little disorganized," Martha said. "He's not all settled in yet."

Betsy petted the rabbit. "Don't you think it looks like Dr. Hunter? They both have such big brown eyes."

Megan nodded. "Everyone seems to know Dr. Hunter."

"He's taken over old Dr. Boyer's practice. Dr. Boyer retired last month and moved to Florida," Martha said, smoothing out the wrinkles in her apron. "My daughter took her little Larissa to Dr. Hunter last week, and she said he was wonderful."

"Anyone know where this wonderful person lives?" Megan asked, shifting the weight of the rabbit to her hip.

"Nicholson Street," Betsy said. "I returned his rabbit two days ago. He's living in the little white cottage across from the cabinetmaker."

Megan set her chin at a determined angle and marched off to do battle with Patrick Hunter. She didn't care if he was Pediatrician of the Month; he had no business fathering a rabbit if he didn't intend to take care of it. Rabbits weren't exactly brilliant. This one probably had a brain the size of a walnut. What were its chances against hordes of tourists and overzealous gardeners? Remember the tragedy of Peter Rabbit's father?

"Don't worry," she told the bunny, "that's not going to happen to you. I'm going to give that Patrick Hunter a piece of my mind."

By the time she reached the Hunter cottage Megan was sweating profusely and had resorted to bundling the enormous rabbit in her cape and slinging it over her shoulder like a sack of potatoes. Lord, she thought, what did he fed this thing, rocks? She stopped at Hunter's front stoop to catch her breath and to reassemble herself and the rabbit into a more dignified appearance.

Before she had the opportunity to unwrap the animal, Patrick Hunter flung his front door open and grinned down at her. "I saw you stomp up my stairs. Is this a social call?"

She swung her cape off her shoulder and into Pat's outstretched arms. "I'm returning your rabbit."

He shook his head at the lumpy black bundle. "I see you've been feeding him again."

Her eyes widened at the sight of a twitching nose and big bunny teeth protruding through a ragged hole in her cape. "Oh, no! Oh, darn!" She glared at Patrick Hunter. "This is all your fault. You should be ashamed of yourself for not taking better care of this rabbit. You don't deserve to have a rabbit. If I had my way I'd have you put in the stockade. What if this sweet thing got lost, or rabbitknapped, or run over?"

Pat took a step backward. Boy, she was really steamed, he thought. He wanted to invite her in for tea, or lust, or something, but he was afraid she might start breaking things . . . like his nose.

She sniffed the air. "I smell something burning."

"My applesauce!" He practically flung the rabbit at her, and ran back into his house.

Megan followed at a distance, closing the door behind her. The cottage, a white clapboard Cape Cod with a gray shake roof and black shutters, was very small. The downstairs consisted of one room, dominated by a walk-in red brick fireplace. Part of the room had been converted into a country kitchen.

She rolled her eyes at the language Pat was aiming at the pot on the stove. "Something go wrong?" she asked.

Pat slouched against the stove with a large, dripping spoon in his hand. "I suppose these things happen."

"Hmmm," she said, "I wouldn't know. I haven't gotten around to learning how to cook. I can toast bread and boil water and defrost most anything, but I can't actually cook." She guessed Patrick Hunter couldn't cook either. A large stainless-steel pot of glop bubbled ominously on the stove, sporadically spewing its contents over the side and onto the floor.

A square wood table sat in the middle of the kitchen area. It was cluttered with sacks of flour and corn meal, a jar of molasses, colonial-style cones of sugar, and a wicker basket filled with sweet potatoes, baking potatoes, and turnips. Several pumpkins sat on the floor beside the table. The counters held jugs of cider, bunches of dried herbs, and loaves of bakery bread. Megan set the rabbit on the floor and motioned to the food.

"Mrs. Hunter likes to cook?"

"No Mrs. Hunter. Just me . . . and Tibbles." He peered into the pot. "Do you think it's done?"

"What is it?"

"Applesauce," he said, sounding insulted.

"What are those big brown lumps?"

"I think that's the part that got a little burned."

Megan wasn't much of a cook, but she'd never made anything that looked as bad as Patrick Hunter's applesauce. She wondered if he misplaced babies at the hospital and melted his rubber gloves in the autoclave.

They both turned when the front door swung open and a young girl timidly entered the room. She wore blue jeans and a denim jacket, and she held a well-swaddled baby in one arm and a brown paper shopping bag in the other.

"I knocked, but nobody heard me," she said. "I couldn't wait any longer. I have to go." Tears clung to her lower lashes and straggled down her cheeks. "I have to go, and I can't take the baby, and I didn't know what to do ... and then I thought of you. I knew you'd take good care of him for me. You and Mrs. Hunter."

She deposited the baby in Megan's arms.

"I'm real sorry I'm in such a rush, but if I don't go now I'll miss my ride. I'll be back as soon as I can. Promise. It won't be any more than two weeks." She kissed the baby, scrubbed at the tears on her cheeks, and ran out the door.

The baby looked up at Megan and started howling.

Megan jiggled the baby. "This kid's *loud*. How do I get it to stop?"

Pat stood motionless, the spoon still in his hand. "Did she say she was leaving the baby with us? Oh, hell!"

He ran out to the sidewalk, looked up and down, jogged half a block down the street, but he couldn't find the girl. He returned to the house and stared in astonishment at Megan, crying with the baby. "Good Lord, what's the matter?"

"I can't get it to stop crying. Just look at the poor little thing. It's all red."

He took the child from her and unwrapped it, slung the baby under his arm, and went back to stirring his applesauce.

"That was Tilly Coogan," he said. "And this is Tim. One of my very first patients."

"Are you related?"'

"Nope."

"Are you . . . um, friends?"

"Nope."

"Why did she give you her baby?"

Pat put a lid on the pot of applesauce and

whistled "Taps." "I guess she thought I'd take good care of him."

"You? The man who burns his applesauce and neglects his rabbit?"

"Yup. I'm a little disorganized, but I'm lovable."

It was true, Megan had to admit, he was lovable. She could hardly keep from squeezing him. She guessed he must stand about six feet, but he didn't look that tall. He had the wide shoulders, slim hips, and hard-muscled arms of an athlete, yet he didn't look like a jock. He looked average. The casually sexy, slightly sloppy version of the boy next door, wearing battered sneakers and threadbare jeans and a gray sweat shirt with the sleeves cut short. And he looked great. He could probably wear his cannibalized sweat shirt to a black-tie dinner and pull it off. Still, pediatrician or not, she wouldn't trust him with a baby.

"What about Tim's father?" she asked.

"No father. Tilly Coogan hasn't had an easy time of it. She's an eighteen-year-old unemployed waitress living in an efficiency apartment over a garage, and I suspect she's been evicted."

15

He rummaged through the paper bag the girl had left and extracted a small pile of freshly laundered, carefully folded baby clothes, two clean baby bottles, and several disposable diapers.

"Looks like we have all the essentials here. I'm going to the office to get Timmy's file, and see if I can track down Tilly. You two guys stay here in case she has a change of heart and comes back."

"You're leaving me here? With the baby?" Megan knew less about babies than she did about cooking. Babies were scary. They cried and drooled and did embarrassing things in their diapers. How had this happened to her?

Pat gently set the baby on the kitchen floor, shrugged into his leather jacket, and grinned at her.

"It isn't as if I'm locking you in the house with Godzilla. You and Tim will get along fine. If he cries just change his diaper or give him a slug of milk. He can't walk yet, but he can crawl. Maybe you should put Tibbles in the outdoor hutch before the Bruiser, here, grabs a hunk of bunny fur."

Megan gave him a dazed look and nodded. "You won't be gone long, will you?"

"What a wench. We hardly know each other, and already you can't get enough of me. Love at first sight, huh?"

He tweaked her freckled nose and smiled as he closed the front door. She had a terrible temper, he thought, couldn't cook, and she didn't know squat about babies, but damned if she didn't look good in his kitchen. All that outrageous hair and eyes the color of a stormy ocean, sort of gray-green, with curly red lashes, and there was an electricity to her. Yessir, he wouldn't mind playing doctor with Megan Murphy.

Megan touched the tip of her finger to the tip of her nose. He'd tweaked her. On the nose. It was the sort of thing someone would to to his child . . . or his rabbit!

Patrick Hunter was a strange person. A total enigma . . . She couldn't tell when he was teasing and when he was serious. He seemed altogether too casual about his responsibilities. And she didn't like being tweaked on the nose in such an offhand manner.

Two hours later Megan was smiling at the

17

little boy sleeping in her arms and wondering why it had taken her so long to discover babies. They were terrific. Timmy was especially terrific—even if he had howled for ages. He had soft blond curls, big blue eyes, and blond eyelashes. His chubby cheeks were flushed in sleep, his pink bow mouth slightly pouted, and his dimpled hand was resting against her breast. She'd pulled the Boston rocker directly in front of the huge brick fireplace, built a blazing inferno, and rocked the child to sleep. The fire had burned itself down to glowing embers, and her arms were stiff from holding the little boy, but she couldn't bring herself to disturb him.

The moment Pat opened the door and saw Megan, he knew he was a goner. Everything about her seemed softened. The flame-red hair was now burnished copper, the ivory skin more golden. She wore a black vest that laced down the front and the scoop-necked, shirred white blouse of a colonial working girl. The costume enhanced the elegant slope of her neck and shoulders and the luscious swell of her breasts.

He'd liked the way she looked in his kitchen,

but he was overwhelmed by the sight of her in his rocking chair. She was the most provocative creature he'd ever encountered. Patrick, he warned himself, she's not the sort to mess with. This was a woman with strong convictions, intense emotions, and morals. Dammit. She had "hands off" written all over her.

He walked over to her and pushed a long, silky strand of hair behind her ear. He wanted to continue touching her until his hands had memorized every square inch of satiny skin.

She looked at him drowsily. "I think my arm is dead."

"Your arm?" he said thickly.

"From holding the baby. I can't feel my fingers any more."

Pat dragged himself back to reality. Here he was, ready to do the caveman thing and drag her off to bed, and she was pinned to the chair by a twenty-two-pound baby. He was losing it. His elevator wasn't going all the way to the top these days. Residency had been too long. He was suffering from social deprivation. He carefully took the baby from her and laid him down on the plump two-cushion couch that served as a room divider.

Megan stood and stretched, rubbing life back into her arm. "Did you find Tilly?"

"No. Her apartment was locked, and she didn't list any relatives on her medical history. I've talked to her neighbors, been to the train station, the bus station, called the airport. She's vanished." Pat set a paper bag on the floor by the fireplace. "I brought us some burgers."

He stoked the embers and added an armful of logs while Megan arranged the fries and shakes and cheeseburgers on the huge brick hearth.

"I can't believe she did this," he said. "She seemed like such a nice kid, and I know she loves this baby."

Megan sat Indian fashion on a red braid rug and took a bite of her cheeseburger. "She must have been desperate."

"No one should ever be that desperate," he said angrily. "This kid is going to become a ward of the state. What the hell was she thinking?"

Megan swallowed, but the cheeseburger felt stuck in her throat. "What do you mean, he'll become a ward of the state? Tilly said she'd only be gone a couple of weeks."

"I can't keep this child. I have to turn him over to the authorities."

"Why? *Why?*"

Oh, boy, Pat thought. He'd seen that look before. It happened shortly after childbirth. As a pediatrician he had a healthy respect for the protective instincts accompanying motherhood, and after two hours of exposure to Timmy Coogan, Megan had obviously caught adoptive hormonal maternalitis. He suspected his chances of prying the kid away from her were zip. He chewed his French fries while he weighed his options.

"He's just a baby, for goodness' sake," she argued. "It isn't as if we found him sleeping in a dumpster. Tilly asked us to take care of him for a little while."

"Us?"

"You. You have to take care of him."

He lounged back on one elbow. "She thought we were married."

Megan felt the blush rise up her neck. The tone of his voice made her uncomfortable. It was a bedroom voice, velvet-edged and suggestive. She slurped her chocolate milk shake and wondered what she was getting into. Patrick Hunter looked like the wolf about to eat the gingerbread man.

"Forget it," she said. "This is one gingerbread man who's going to make it to old age."

"You want to run that by me again?"

She stuffed her empty wrappers into the bag. "No. It would be embarrassing. I'm going home."

He followed her to the kitchen. "Hold on. You can't leave me alone with the baby."

"Sure, I can."

"I'll turn him over to the state."

"You wouldn't!"

"I have no choice. I work all day. What would I do with him?"

"You could get a baby-sitter."

Gotcha, Pat thought. He'd gotten her back in his kitchen. Back in his rocking chair. And who knew where they'd go from the rocking chair?

"Okay. I'll let you baby-sit, but only if you agree to have supper with us every night. I think it's important for a family to be together at the dinner table."

Megan smiled triumphantly and wrapped her cape around her shoulders. "Deal!"

She whisked out the front door and headed

for her car, parked by Merchants Square. She'd walked less than a block when she stopped short and gasped. Patrick Hunter had manipulated her! That no-good, irresistible skunk had wheedled her into taking care of the baby!

Chapter 2

Megan opened one eye and squinted at the clock radio. Five-thirty in the morning, and some lunatic was pounding on her front door. She dragged herself out of bed and looked out her bedroom window. She was right. It was a lunatic. It was Patrick Hunter. She opened her window and yelled down at him. "If you want to live you'll stop pounding on my front door."

"Cranky in the morning, huh? I know how to fix that."

She might be cranky, but she wasn't stupid. She knew exactly what he meant, and she was going to ignore it. "What are you doing here?"

He held up a blue plaid bundle for her inspection. "The baby."

"It's five-thirty in the morning!"

"I have to be at the hospital by six."

Megan blinked, nodded, and slammed the window shut. She shuffled into a pair of big blue furry slippers and halfheartedly slid a blue velour robe over her long silk nightgown.

"Hospital by six," she mumbled as she scuffed down the stairs. She flicked the light on in the foyer and unlatched the front door. "I'm not a morning person," she explained to Pat.

He handed her the sleeping baby and retrieved two grocery bags from his car. "That was before motherhood, Mrs. Hunter."

Mrs. Hunter, she thought. Very funny. She awkwardly held the baby in front of her as she headed for the kitchen. "I don't remember how to hold him."

Pat followed her. "You act like you've never seen a baby before."

"Not up close. I was an only child. I was spoiled and pampered and never exposed to the sordid aspects of life . . . like drool and baby poo."

He set a pile of baby clothes on the counter, deposited a gallon of milk in the refrigerator, stacked up a few jars of baby food, and slapped a hastily scribbled note on the kitchen table.

"I've jotted down a few helpful hints. And just in case life gets sordid . . ." He took a huge box of disposable diapers from the second bag and set it on the floor.

She closed her eyes and thought of an appropriate expletive. "I don't know how to do this," she wailed. "I can't change a diaper!"

Pat unwrapped the baby and spread the blue plaid blanket on the floor. He removed Tim's heavy sweater and knitted hat, leaving him in yellow terry-cloth pajamas, and sat him in the middle of the blanket. Then he rummaged through the kitchen drawers, finding two wooden spoons, a plastic measuring cup, and a medium-size saucepan. "Toys," he told Megan, placing them on the blanket with Tim. "If you have any problems, my office number is on the paper."

"How did you find me?"

"My receptionist. She's lived here all her life and knows everything about everyone."

"Did she tell you I have a job? What about *my* job? How am I supposed to work?"

"You only work on weekends. Today is Monday."

"Wrong. Being a visitors' aide is a weekend

job. I'm just doing that temporarily to make money. My real job is—"

"You should have thought of all this before you begged me to let you baby-sit." Pat bent down and kissed Tim on the top of his head. "Good-bye, Tim. Be a good guy for Mommy Hunter." He turned to Megan and kissed her on the top of the head too. "Good-bye, Mrs. Hunter."

She narrowed her eyes. "I hate when you do that!"

"Do what?"

"Tweak my nose or kiss the top of the head . . . or wherever."

Pat looked down at her. In all honesty he wasn't that happy about tweaking her on the nose or kissing her on top of the head, either, but he was just about foaming at the mouth to kiss her on her wherever. She'd been too sleepy and too distracted to belt her robe, and in the course of her travels about the house it had parted, exposing a tantalizing corridor of smooth skin and slinky nightgown. He had been making a supreme effort not to stare. He was afraid if he got a really good look, he might start drooling, and he knew she hated drool.

"Megan . . ." He studied her face, unsure of the emotions he found there. She was lovely. Already she was tying him in knots, yet he didn't have a clue about her feelings for him. He suspected they might not be flattering. His gaze strayed to the low neckline of her pale yellow nightgown. Oh, hell, he thought, sliding his hands along her neck. It would be worth a broken nose to get a good-morning kiss.

Megan stood absolutely still at the touch of his hands, barely breathing, wondering at the sensations flooding through her, a paralyzing mixture of desire, guilt, and anger. There was something else, too, a ridiculous delusion that she actually was Mrs. Hunter.

It felt perfectly natural to be standing in her nightgown and robe, waiting for Pat to kiss her. She tipped her head toward him and instinctively parted her lips, thinking that he was really very nice in the morning. Warm and cuddly, with that endearing, teasing grin. She watched him slowly move closer and felt his lips barely skim across hers. Much better than getting tweaked on the nose, she thought dreamily. This wasn't a boring, taken-for-granted kiss. This was a friendly kiss.

His hands slid down her arms and she was suddenly crushed to him. His hands moved across her back. He whispered her name and kissed her ear, then her neck just below the earlobe. She gasped at her body's fiery reaction. She hadn't expected this. Not so fast. Not so intense.

"Whoa," she said, pushing against him. "Time out. Just a darn minute."

He stared at her in a haze of desire. "Whoa?"

"You have some nerve, having an innocent little nose like that and then kissing like Conan the Barbarian." She swallowed and put her hand to her chest to help keep her heart from breaking through the skin. "And in front of the baby! What will he think?"

Shoot, Pat thought. Now he'd done it. He'd attacked her like some kind of animal. Hunter, he silently shouted, you're such a weenie! He wrapped the blue robe tightly around her and tied the belt in a double knot, then looked at his watch.

"Damn, I'm late. I'll pick up the kid at six."

He bolted through the doorway, then paused. "About that kiss. I don't want you to think I'm easy."

"I don't think you're easy. I think you're nuts. I think you're a sex maniac."

He grinned and waved. "Good. I was worried."

She listened to his car pull out of the driveway and turned to the sleeping Tim. "You know what I really think? I think he's magic. No one's ever kissed me like that. *No one!* Not that it matters. I'm done with men, forever."

She put the water on for coffee and sat down to read the helpful hints, but her thoughts kept returning to Pat. She wondered if she was just licking her wounds from her relationship with Dave. Was this just a reaction from her bruised ego? No, she thought. When Pat had touched her, it had been magical. No other explanation. She'd gone gooney-brained.

Tim awoke, saw the strange woman looking down at him, and began to howl.

Almost twelve hours later Megan glared at Tim and wiped a splot of smushed green beans off her nose. The baby seemed to have become adjusted to her during this long day.

"So, how old are you, kid? Nine, ten months?

You think you're a match for a twenty-seven-year-old college graduate? Hah! Gotcha."

She successfully spooned a load of green beans into the little mouth.

"Brrrph," Tim said, spewing green beans across the table and into Megan's hair.

Pat chugged into the driveway in his old tan Dodge van and made a quick assessment of Megan's house in the fading light. He'd found out she was house-sitting for a member of the William and Mary faculty who was on sabbatical. On the outskirts of town, the house was surrounded by several acres of land. A barn and a large fenced-in pasture stood behind it. It was a neat two-story colonial, painted a traditional Williamsburg butternut yellow, with trim in two shades of green. A battered car was parked by the garage. The car was a faded maroon color, and was missing a back bumper and a front left fender. Possibly the only car in Williamsburg uglier than his, he thought.

He let himself into the unlocked house. "Hello," he called from the front door. "Anybody home?"

"In the kitchen."

"Having fun?"

She scowled at him as he walked into the kitchen, and pointed at her green-speckled hair. "You think this is fun?"

Pat made an effort not to laugh. Being a new mother could be a trying experience.

Megan leaned back in her chair. "Well, I suppose it has been fun. You know what he did today? He said cookie. This kid is so smart." She wiped Timmy's face clean with a wet cloth.

"The problem is, I'm not getting anything done! This is a busy time of the year for me." She lifted a teapot from the counter and handed it to Pat. "I'm a potter. I make these tea sets, and a little boutique in Old Town Alexandria sells them for me. They have a big order in for the Christmas season."

"You made this? It's beautiful."

She took it from him and ran her finger over the white-and-blue glaze. "Thanks. My really pretty pieces I save for a gallery in Washington. I'm going to have my first one-woman show in January."

Pat looked at the little boy tied to a kitchen chair with an apron and felt guilty. He hadn't known about Megan's pottery. Somehow he had to make things easier for her. "Maybe I should hire a different baby-sitter. I didn't realize you had these commitments."

Megan noticed he was wearing the sneakers with the sutures again. He didn't have any money, she guessed. He was just starting out, like her, and he was probably getting by day to day. Where would he find the money to pay a baby-sitter? Besides, she liked Timmy. She wouldn't trust just anyone to take care of him. She shook her head and opened a jar of beige gook.

"No way. We made a deal. This kid doesn't get to spit beans on anybody but me . . . or you. Here." She handed the gook to Pat. "You get to feed him dessert. Rice pudding."

"Looks pretty good. Do we have an extra jar? I didn't have time for lunch."

"Sorry. We have junior beef stew and smashed beets." She looked in her freezer. "Turkey dinner, ham and sweet potato, veal parmigiana."

"Veal parmigiana. You weren't kidding when you said you couldn't cook? Do you always eat frozen dinners?"

"No. Mostly I eat peanut-butter-and-jelly sandwiches. Why is this kid eating his food for you? Why isn't he decorating your face with it?"

"Would you spit out dessert?"

Pat certainly had chosen the right profession, Megan thought as she sat down across from him. He was great with babies.

"Are you a pediatrician because you know a lot about kids? Or do you know a lot about kids because you're a pediatrician?"

"A little bit of both. I have an older brother and three younger sisters. I guess I did my share of baby-sitting."

"Do they live around here?"

"My parents live in San Diego. My brother and his wife and kids live in Connecticut. My oldest sister is a graduate student at Berkeley. My two younger sisters go to UCLA." He grimaced. "Everyone's coming here for Thanksgiving."

"Oh, boy."

"It seemed like a good idea two weeks ago. A real, old-fashioned Thanksgiving in Williamsburg." He thunked the spoon into the empty pudding jar and stared at the steaming frozen dinner she slid in front of him. "You sure you don't know how to cook?"

"I know better than to burn applesauce."

"That puts you one up on me, Mrs. Hunter. Welcome aboard."

"What do you mean, 'Welcome aboard'?"

"We're a family. You're Mrs. Hunter. What would people say if we didn't spend Thanksgiving together?"

"I'm *not* Mrs. Hunter. We're *not* a family. I don't give a flying moneky what people say—"

"Please."

It was the first time she'd seen him totally serious, and it left her speechless. His eyes were unsettling when they were teasing, but they were devastating when they were serious, and he'd spoken in a husky whisper that could have pursuaded her to do almost anything.

Pat was even more surprised than Megan. The unnerving truth was that he couldn't imagine a Thanksgiving without her. He knew it was crazy, but he actually thought of her as Mrs. Hunter. He suspected it was because all day he'd been fantasizing about her performing wifely functions—most of them in her satiny nightgown.

A real, old-fashioned Thanksgiving with Pat and his family and little Timmy, Megan mused. The more she thought about it, the more excited she became. It would be wonderful to have a Thanksgiving feast in the little restored house with the huge fireplace.

"Are you really going to make all your own food?"

"Will you help me?"

"Of course I'll help you. It'll be great. We can have pumpkin pie and homemade cranberry sauce and spoon bread."

Pat poked at his veal. It was still frozen inside. "Do you honestly think we can cook a real meal?"

"Piece of cake."

Timmy slumped down, still bound to the back of the chair with the apron. His eyes were closed in sleep and his mouth was slightly parted.

Megan and Pat smiled as they shared a moment of parental affection.

"I think I should be getting him to bed," Pat said, untying the sleeping child while Megan got the big blue blanket. He wanted to bed Megan, too, but he didn't think that would be such an easy task.

She wrapped Timmy in the blanket and handed Pat his jacket. "Don't even think about it," she said.

"You read minds?"

"That thought was pretty clear. Don't get carried away with this Mrs. Hunter stuff. I'm through with men."

He studied her for a moment. Her expression was somber. "Through with men forever?"

"Forever."

"You're not . . . um, you know."

She blushed. "No. I'm completely heterosexual, and I'm absolutely healthy. It's just that I've decided marriage isn't my cup of tea."

Pat had an invitation for casual sex on the tip of his tongue when he realized that wasn't what he wanted. He didn't even want to joke about it. Did that mean he was falling in love? This was serious, he thought. This was depressing. How the hell had this happened? The rabbit. He was going home to strangle the rabbit.

He shifted Tim to one arm and scowled at Megan. "Are you going to wear that sexy nightgown again tonight?"

"No. I'm wearing long underwear and a flannel granny gown. An ugly one."

"Good," he said through clenched teeth. He cradled her neck in his free hand, kissed her full on the lips, and left, slamming the door behind him.

Megan stood in the empty foyer and wondered how she'd managed to lose control of her life so easily. One minute everything was clean and uncomplicated, and then, *wham*, her mind was cluttered with babies and sexy pediatricians and roast turkeys. The worst part was that she was actually enjoying all this. Megan, you're such a jerk, she told herself. Have you forgotten about the bag hanging in the closet upstairs? Have you forgotten about Dave? And what about Steve? And Jimmy Fee, the little nerd?

Okay, she thought, she'd allow one man into her life. Tim. The other man would henceforth be referred to as "Dr. Hunter." And no more of that Mrs. Hunter stuff. And no more kisses! She'd set her alarm tonight, and tomorrow she'd get up at five o'clock and be fully clothed before Dr. Hunter arrived.

Chapter 3

Megan's eyes flew open, and she sat bolt upright in bed. She snatched the small clock radio from her nightstand and squinted at the green digital numbers. Five-thirty, and Patrick Hunter was pounding on her front door. Damn! She must have shut the alarm off in her sleep.

She threw the window open and shouted, "Hold your pants on, for crying out loud. I'll be right there." And she'd be dressed, too, she thought. No more repetitions of the morning before.

She stepped into navy sweat pants, tucked her pink satin nightgown into the elastic waistband, and shuffled, half asleep, down the stairs.

Pat stood in the open doorway and gaped at her. She was wearing another one of those slippery, man-eating nightgowns. This time it was a delicate pink, and she had it tucked into a pair of sweats. He licked his lips and nervously cleared his throat, but he couldn't stop staring.

She swayed drowsily and looked at him through half-closed eyes. "Well," she said, "I guess it's morning again." The thin strap to her nightgown slid off her left shoulder, exposing yet another half inch of soft, smooth skin.

Pat almost dropped the baby. "Oh, Lord, Megan," he muttered, "how am I supposed to behave when you look like that?"

She looked down at herself and sighed heavily. "Shoot. I forgot the top half of the sweats. I'll be right back." She lumbered up the stairs. "Mornings. I hate mornings."

By the time she got to her bedroom she'd forgotten what she intended to do there, so she went back to bed.

Pat looked at his watch. Megan had been gone for ten minutes, and he didn't hear any movement overhead. He'd made coffee and dragged a vanful of baby stuff into her house and still . . . no Megan. "Megan?" he called up the stairs. Nothing. "Megan, did you go back to bed?"

Megan Murphy in bed, he thought. What a rotten break. Now he'd have to go wake her up. Just like Prince Charming. Maybe she'd be so sound asleep, he'd have to resort to something more drastic than a kiss. Maybe she wasn't asleep at all. Maybe this was just a ruse to get him up to her bedroom. Of course! Lord, he was so dense. Why else would she answer the door in her sexy nightgown? She wanted him. She probably hadn't slept all night, thinking about his kisses, and now she was ready to be loved. All right!

He laid the sleeping Tim safely on the floor, climbed the stairs, took his tennis shoes off, left his leather jacket draped over the banister, loosened his tie, and opened the top button on his blue pin-striped shirt.

He paused at her open bedroom door, marveling at her shining hair spread across her pillow. "Megan?"

She turned and stretched in her sleep. The quilt slipped low, revealing an alabaster shoulder and the tempting swell of her breast. Pat watched her for a moment. "Hey, Mrs. Hunter," he whispered.

"Mmrph," she answered.

He sat on the edge of the bed. Lifting a silky fall of hair from her face, he leaned forward and kissed her lightly on her sleep-softened lips. She opened her eyes.

"Sexy lady," he said, in a low, raspy voice.

Sexy lady? she repeated silently. What the heck was that supposed to mean? She grabbed at the covers and pulled them up to her neck. "What are you doing on my bed? Did you just kiss me?"

Pat felt the scalding heat rise from his shirt collar. "I thought . . . Oh, hell."

Her sweat shirt was draped over a chair by the window. He ripped the covers off the bed, yanked her to her feet, and pulled the sweat shirt over her head.

"I've made you a pot of coffee. It's in the kitchen. You remember where the kitchen is? That room downstairs? The baby is in the living room on the floor."

He swore under his breath and gathered her into his arms, then kissed her as if she were a rare delicacy to be savored and leisurely enjoyed. He held her at arm's length and pressed his lips together. "Well," he said huskily.

She swayed toward him. "Well," she parroted just as huskily.

What a confusing mess this was, he thought. Megan was all bristly one minute, then warm and responsive the next. She was driving him nuts.

"I have to go. I sent out a distress call last night and was able to gather up some stuff to make your life with Tim more workable. Also, I left a key to my house on the kitchen counter. I have office hours until eight o'clock tonight. Would you mind putting Timmy to bed and staying with him until I get home?"

She nodded numbly, wondering who was ultimately going to get put to bed.

"You're not going back to sleep, are you?"

"Not me. I have work to do. Work, work, work."

She watched while Pat let himself out the front door, then she padded into the kitchen. A nylon mesh playpen sat in the middle of her kitchen floor. A cardboard box filled with toys and a new giant box of disposable diapers sat on the floor beside the playpen. A collapsible stroller stood in one corner, along with a shopping bag of used but clean baby clothes and a navy diaper bag. On her kitchen counter were jars of baby food, boxes of cereal, graham crackers, juice, and a single, perfect flame-red rose.

He'd brought her a rose. What a crummy thing to do, she thought. How was she supposed to remain indifferent to him when he brought her roses and made her morning coffee?

Timmy woke up and let out a wail, and she rushed to the living room and picked him up. After kissing and cuddling him until he cooed, she carried him back to the kitchen.

"This isn't fair, is it?" she asked Timmy. "The good doctor is cute and sexy . . . and now he's nice! I can't deal with this. I'm only human. Why couldn't the lousy rabbit belong to someone mean and stupid?"

She put Tim into the playpen and poured herself a cup of coffee. Then she put the rose in a bud vase, grudgingly admitting to herself that she was inordinately pleased.

Good thing her parents had moved to Florida, she mused. They'd take one look at Dr. Hunter and never stop hounding her. They meant well, but they were partially the reason for the Dave disaster. And they were definitely the instigators of the Steve fiasco. Lately, their hysteria had been traveling right over the phone wires. She was twenty-seven and didn't even have a boyfriend. The end of the world. She could hear her parents nervously cracking their knuckles all the way from Florida.

"You'd think they'd learn," she said to Tim, waving her arms. "Some women aren't meant to get married."

She carried the box of toys to the small outbuilding she'd converted into a pottery studio. Returning to the kitchen, she slung Tim under one arm and grabbed the playpen with the other. "This is going to be great, kiddo. I'm going to teach you how to make a teapot."

At six-thirty Megan let herself into Pat's house on Nicholson Street and took an unhurried tour. The small cottage was part of the historic area. It wasn't one of the eighty-eight buildings still standing from the eighteenth and nineteenth centuries, but it had been accurately reconstructed from its original eighteenth-century foundation. The exterior shell was precisely as it would have been in colonial times, and the interior had been adapted only slightly to modern living.

Megan wondered how Pat had been lucky enough to get the little house. The private residences in the historic area were occupied, for the most part, by employees of Colonial Williamsburg, and the houses were at a premium.

She knew this particular house had originally been an outbuilding, an eighteenth-century kitchen, and it still maintained that warm, country-kitchen feeling. The downstairs floor was wide plank, the walls creamy white with dark wood cupboards. One entire wall was devoted to the large brick fireplace and step-up hearth. A small pewter-and-candle chandelier hung directly over the front entrance. A larger chandelier had been placed in the middle of the room.

The room was partially divided by the mahogany staircase leading to the upstairs. The small nook it created had been converted into a modern kitchen. A plump couch covered in a brick red and creamy white check faced the fireplace. A red braid throw rug covered the living-room-area floor, and a rocking chair sat invitingly close to the fireplace. Houseplants had been set in copper pots and wooden tubs. Megan thought it was the perfect Thanksgiving room. It practically shouted pumpkin pie and roast turkey.

She tugged Timmy out of his new snowsuit and selected a dog-eared book from the diaper bag to read to him. She struck a match to the kindling in the fireplace and settled herself in the rocking chair with the baby on her lap.

"You're going to like this," she said to Timmy. "It's about a little red hen. You like little red hens?"

Timmy sucked his thumb vigorously and watched her with big blue eyes.

"Good. Me too. When we're done with the book I'll give you some juice and then it's bedtime."

More than two hours later Pat found Megan in his kitchen up to her elbows in pie dough. She was wearing a pair of tight jeans, white sneakers, and an aquamarine sweater with a loose turtleneck, and the sleeves were pushed high on her arms. Her hair curled in wiry tendrils around her flushed face and cascaded over her shoulders in lush waves. Flour smudged her face and her jeans.

She turned to him and smiled and laughed, and he heard his heart give one great *thud*. She was a perfect snowflake, a summer sunset, a wave breaking on virgin sand. She was exquisite, with a beauty that defied age and fashion. She was a woman, filled with life and vitality. The sexiest strumpet ever created, he thought, feeling a smile tug at his mouth.

He draped his jacket over a kitchen chair and peered into a big stainless-steel bowl on the table. "What's this brown stuff?"

"Pumpkin. I'm making a pumpkin pie!"

He stood as close as he could without touching her and tried not to smile too broadly. "You're a mess."

"I've had some problems." She took a step back and bumped into the counter. Suddenly the kitchen was very small and much warmer. "The pumpkin stuff was easy, but the pie crust . . . Have you ever made pie crust?"

He took off his tie and undid the top two buttons on his shirt. Little black hairs curled from the open V. "Nope. I've never made pie crust. Do you think it's warm in here?"

"I have the oven on, and the fire is going, and . . ." And her heart was racing, she thought. If he didn't kiss her she was going to tear his shirt off and pin him to the kitchen floor. No! she shouted silently. That was wrong. That was *not* what she was going to do. Remember the bag? Remember Dave? She hit herself on the head with the wooden spoon.

Pat's eyes widened. "Why'd you do that?"

"I deserved it." She waved his question away and returned to her pie crust. "This is the third crust I've made. The first one had too much water and got slimy. The second one I rolled out too thin and it stuck to the rolling pin and my shirt. This one is going to be perfect. Look, it's almost round!"

Pat moved the pie plate closer to the dough, and together they maneuvered the crust into the pan. "Damn!" he said, his voice filled with admiration. "You did it. You made a pie crust." He gave her a quick kiss on the lips. "I'm proud of you."

Their gazes locked for a moment while they each pondered taking the kiss a step further.

"No," Megan said.

"Yes," Pat said. He pressed himself against her, snaking his arms around her waist.

"I'm serious."

"Me too. Want to get married?"

"No!"

"Want to go to bed?"

She narrowed her eyes and wrinkled her nose. "You want to get conked with my wooden spoon?"

"You didn't answer my question."

"Hmmm." Of course she wanted to go to bed with him, she thought. If her attraction to him continued to grow, she might even want to marry him. Unfortunately, it was all impossible, and what she really *didn't* want to do was fall in love with him. That would be totally painful.

"Hmmm?" he repeated. "That's encouraging." He brushed his hips lightly against hers.

She wanted to be encouraging, she thought. She also wanted to erase the threat of nuclear war, eliminate hunger from the face of the earth, and find a cure for cancer. Unfortunately, none of those things was within her power.

She placed the palms of her hands on his

chest and pushed firmly. "I'm going to finish my pie, and you're going to do the dishes, and then we're going to sit down and talk." He was much too lovable, and she was far too susceptible to his charms. She didn't want to bare her soul to him, but he had to be made to understand that this was a working friendship, not a love affair. They were briefly bound together by Timmy and Thanksgiving. She didn't want to jeopardize either of those things, but she was not going to bed with him.

She fluted the edge of the crust, just as the cookbook showed, and poured the filling into the shell. Turning toward the oven, she allowed herself a moment of sexist ogling as she watched Pat, his back to her, rinse the dishes and load them into the dishwasher. His shirt sleeves were rolled to above his elbows, displaying strong, muscular arms. Despite the rigors of med school, he'd managed to keep in shape. He was nearly perfect, with broad shoulders, trim waist, a hard, flat stomach, and slim hips. His faded jeans clung to the world's sexiest buns. She tried to picture him naked, but there were a few details beyond her imagination. She sighed wistfully and put the pie in the oven.

Pat stowed the last bowl in the dishwasher and dried his hands on a kitchen towel. "Okay, what are we going to talk about?" he asked, reaching for her.

She sidled away, putting the kitchen table between them. "Us. Mostly you."

He leaned against the counter and lazily folded his arms across his chest. His expression was serious, but his eyes were glinting with pleasure as he gazed at her. "What about me?"

"You're very attractive."

"And?"

"And I like you. You're fun, and you're great with Timmy, and you're nice to me."

His gaze didn't waver, but his voice dropped an octave. "I like you, too, and I have an uncomfortable feeling this conversation is about to turn around."

"The simple truth is that you don't fit into my future. At least, not in a romantic way. I'd like to think of you as a friend. A very *platonic* friend."

The corners of his mouth tightened almost imperceptibly, and his brown eyes darkened.

"I'd like to think of you as a friend. I'd also like to think of you as a lover."

She pressed her lips together. "You're not cooperating."

He unfolded his arms and walked toward her. "Nope."

She edged around the table. "How dare you just disregard my feelings? I've been totally honest with you."

"And I'm being honest with you. I want you, Megan Murphy. And I'm going to do everything I can to get you."

"Holy cow." Megan knew it was a dumb exclamation, but her mind was the texture of Timmy's rice pudding. Her body was in a state of hormonal riot, and her mind had completely shut down. No one had ever said anything like that to her before.

"Maybe we should dump the honest approach," she said, reaching for her fleece-lined jean jacket, slipping her arms into the sleeves while she moved toward the door. "Maybe I should go home now." If she could, she silently added. Move, legs, *move!*

Pat closed the space between them. He took her jacket lapels in his hands and gently pressed her against the front door. "Not going to stay for pie?"

"This isn't fair," she said thickly. "You have a bogus nose."

He grinned down at her. "A bogus nose?"

"It's the sort of perfect little nose you find on the boy next door. It's ... um, innocent. I shouldn't have paid any attention to it. I should have sized you up by your backside. You have a killer behind."

A killer behind! he thought. He couldn't wait to go upstairs and take a look at it in the mirror. All these years he'd assumed his smile was his best feature, and now he found out he had a killer behind. "Say good night, Gracie."

"Good night," Megan whispered.

He buttoned her jacket, letting his fingers brush against her breasts as he worked his way down. Then he leaned against her and kissed her deeply and slowly. "See you in the morning," he said, opening the front door.

Megan took a step backward into the cold night and shivered. The next morning she was going to answer the door fully dressed, she vowed, even if it meant staying up all night or sleeping in her clothes.

Pat rested his forehead against the closed door and decided that the next morning was an eternity away. And it would take him that long to understand Megan Murphy. So many contradictions and secrets, and he was totally enthralled by her.

"Hunter," he said, "you're in deep trouble."

Chapter 4

The historic district of Williamsburg was roughly the shape of a long rectangle. At the west end of the rectangle was a small commercial shopping area, Merchants Square. Just beyond that, at the very end of Duke of Gloucester Street, sat William and Mary College. On Friday afternoon, Megan parked in the Merchants Square parking lot and pulled the collapsible stroller from the back seat of the big maroon car. She set Timmy in it, adjusted his harness, and gave him the new yellow blanket Pat had bought.

During summer months Merchants Square was filled with people browsing through the shops and eating at the outdoor cafés. Today, the sky was winter gray, the wind whipped Megan's hair across her face, and the tourists browsed at a rather fast pace. The stroller clattered over the brick sidewalk as Megan headed for North Boundary Street.

She tucked her flyaway hair into the collar of her navy pea coat and reread the address she'd written on a slip of paper. Turning left off North Boundary, she began looking for house numbers in a neighborhood of small bungalows, which were rented mostly by students and a few young faculty members. She stopped at a large gray clapboard house and studied the dark windows of the small apartment over the attached garage. A ripple of unidentifiable emotion passed through her. Fear? Anger? Relief? She didn't know what she felt. She lifted Timmy from the stroller and walked to the outside stairs leading to Tilly Coogan's apartment.

"What do you think, Tim? You think Mommy's home?"

Timmy held the blanket tight to his chest. "Mum," he jabbered.

Megan pressed her lips together. Mum had flown the coop, she thought grimly. Mum was nowhere to be found. She wondered if Timmy knew that. It was only natural that he missed his mother, and yet he seemed like a happy, well-adjusted child. Megan supposed children were flexible at this age. Or perhaps it was a reflection of Timmy's personality that he could take things in stride.

She knew it was an empty gesture, but she knocked on the apartment door anyway. There was no answer, and she tried the door and the window beside it. Both were locked. There had been no word from Tilly, and Megan was worried. She was beginning to wonder if the girl would return. After caring for Timmy for five days, she couldn't understand how Tilly could have left him, even for an hour.

She took a stack of letters from the black metal mailbox and riffled through a week's worth of junk mail. Tilly Coogan must have led a lonely existence in Williamsburg, she thought. No one to take in the mail, and only letters addressed to "Occupant." She stood looking at the blank window for a few minutes, as if at any time a light might be switched on or the phone would ring. Neither of those things happened, and Megan finally turned with a sigh and walked back to Duke of Gloucester Street.

At five o'clock the twilight was heavy over

the darkened buildings. Duke of Gloucester Street was almost empty as the shops closed for the day and the lantern-style streetlights blinked on. Megan paused briefly at Bruton Parish Church and listened to the faint strains of organ music.

Her life had always been very secure, she realized. The little brick house in South River, New Jersey, had been a lot like the practical pig's house. It had held up against all the huffing and puffing of childhood. Her father had been a policeman. In South River that was as safe as being a shoe salesman, and only slightly more prestigious. Her mother was a housewife, plain and simple. It was what she wanted to do, and she did it well. They'd had a twenty-foot Criscraft in their driveway and a gas barbecue in their back yard. Her father had regarded growing grass as a moral obligation, right up there with church on Sunday and sparkling white socks on Monday.

Megan's finely arched brows drew together in a frown. She'd spent her whole life worrying about freckles, for crying out loud. This poor kid in the stroller didn't have a father. He didn't have a little brick house. He didn't even have a mother anymore. He had Megan and Pat, and that fact raised frightening questions in Megan's mind . . . questions without answers.

She continued past the miller and the silversmith. Anne Hedgeworth stood on the steps of the wigmaker's shop and waved. She wore a white ruffled pinner, a colonial headdress, and an apricot dress with lace at the shoulders and cuffs. Megan waved back, marveling at how Anne always looked so attractive in the fancier costume of the Williamsburg upper class. At the end of the day, Anne's stomacher was precisely buttoned and her pinner in place, an accomplishment Megan suspected she could never achieve.

"There'd always be a button popped at my waist from too many sugar cookies," she told Timmy. "And I can't manage a mobcap. What would I ever do with a pinner? Anne looks pretty, but I think I'm destined to be a peasant."

She turned at the alley leading to the Raleigh Tavern Bake Shop. The bakery was closed for the day, and inside two women bustled about, cleaning trays and packing away Sally Lunn loaves and Queen Ann tarts. They saw Megan and Timmy looking in the window and hurried over with a cookie for Timmy.

Getting a free cookie at five o'clock had become a ritual for Timmy and Megan. For the past three days she had taken Timmy for a walk along the quiet streets, gotten a cookie from the women at the bakery, and gone to Patrick's house to share the evening meal. Usually it was a disaster. Gray chicken cooked in the microwave. French fries that bubbled over and set the stove on fire. Thank goodness they hadn't burned the house down. The night before, they'd made shoe-leather steak. Tonight they were playing it safe with canned chicken noodle soup and bagels with cream cheese.

It was five-thirty when Megan reached Pat's little white house. The air over Nicholson Street was fragrant with the smoke from blazing fireplaces, and the windows of private residences glowed golden in the encroaching darkness. Usually she was the first to arrive at Pat's, but today the lights were shining in every window, upstairs and down, and the cheerfully lit house reminded Megan of a giant jack-o'-lantern.

Pat was setting the table. He looked up and grinned when she opened the door. "Hope you're hungry. I've gone to all the trouble of opening a can and slicing a bagel."

He wore jeans with a hole in the knee and a powder-blue-and-white rugby shirt, and Megan thought he looked much more tasty than the soup he was heating. She took off Timmy's coat and put him in the high chair. "You're home early."

"Had some cancellations." He filled Timmy's three-section baby plate with green gook, red gook, and brown lumpy gunk.

Megan grimaced when Pat handed her the spoon. "Do I have to do this?"

"I did it last night."

"Is that red gook smashed beets?"

"Yup."

She reluctantly sat opposite Timmy. "This isn't fair. I hate smashed beets. He had smashed beets for lunch yesterday, and it took two showers to get them out of my hair."

Pat had a sexy rejoinder to make about showers, but he bit his tongue. He'd been very careful since Tuesday night. He'd declared his intentions, and now he was waiting. Not very patiently, he admitted, but he was determined to give Megan a few days to get to know him. Besides, falling in love was more than sex. It was conversation at the dinner table, confidences shared, support offered, and comfortable quiet times. His mind knew this to be true, but his body was pushing for sex.

Timmy plunged his fist into the red gook, and smashed beets flew everywhere.

Megan didn't even blink. She'd been through all this before. Beets dripped from her nose and clung to her hair. Her khaki safari shirt looked as if it had measles. Pat turned back to the soup, but Megan could see his shoulders shaking with silent laughter. She smiled stiffly and offered Timmy a spoonful of beans. He ate three spoonfuls and sneezed. Now Megan had green interspersed with red.

Pat wiped the beets off her face. "It's not so bad, honey. It looks . . . colorful. Needs a little orange, though. Maybe I should give you some squash."

"I'm going to give you squash in a minute. I'm going to squash your nose."

"You wouldn't want to do that," he said, trying to look serious. "It's so cute."

"Hmmm. You think your nose is cute?"

"I know it's cute. My whole face is cute. You can't imagine how awful it is to be thirty years old and still be cute." He set a plate of carrot sticks and green-pepper slices on the table. "Old ladies stop me in the supermarket and pinch my cheek."

"That is pretty terrible."

He munched on a carrot. "I always wanted to be handsome, masculine, enigmatic—but I ended up cute."

He was all those things, Megan thought. When you got to know him, he was handsome and incredibly masculine and even enigmatic. Cute was just a first impression that later gave way to more complicated qualities. She gave Timmy a bottle of milk and took his supper plate to the sink. She poured herself a glass of orange juice, turned toward the table, and stepped in a splotch of beets.

"Yow!" she shouted as she slid across the floor. She landed with a solid thud on her rear.

Pat studied her now juice-soaked shirt. "I was only kidding about the orange. You really didn't have to go to all this trouble."

She pressed her lips together and glared at him.

"Are you okay?" he asked belatedly. "Did you get hurt?"

"I'm fine, but I'm disgusting. I never realized being a mother was so dangerous."

He gently helped her to her feet, then put his arm around her shoulders and steered her to the stairs. "I have a great idea. How about if you take a nice, hot, relaxing shower, wash all the beans away, get dressed in one of my clean shirts, and I'll mop up the floor?"

She dug her heels in at the foot of the stairs. "Wait a minute. Is this a trick to get me up to your bedroom in a naked condition?"

"That's insulting. Boy, that really hurts. What kind of a person do you think I am?"

"Desperate? Perverted? Lecherous?"

"Besides that?"

Megan smiled at him. He wasn't desperate, perverted, or lecherous. He'd been very nice. For three days now he'd been a perfect gentleman. A little too perfect, she admitted. She missed getting swept off her feet by his passionate kisses. She knew it was all for the best, yet still, it had become a tad frustrating. It was like waiting for an earthquake that never happened. You were relieved, but you were also strangely disappointed.

Ten minutes later, she stepped out of the small upstairs bathroom and admired Pat's bedroom while she towel-dried her hair. These two rooms occupied the entire top floor of the cottage. The bedroom was directly under the eaves, so that the roof sloped on two sides, and two dormer windows looked out on the street. Window seats had been built into the alcoves, and their chintz teal cushions matched the puffy down quilt on the queen-size cherry-wood four-poster. The upper half of the room was papered in a small, Williamsburg teal-and-cream print. Below the chair rail the walls were painted creamy white. Two large pewter-and-glass chimneyed candlesticks sat on the low cherry dresser.

It was the most romantic bedroom Megan had ever seen. It was a room for loving long into the night, she thought dreamily, until the candles were melted stubs and the lovers were sated and comfortably entwined under the feather quilt. She had such a strong feeling of belonging in the room that the thought of Pat lying under the quilt without her brought a painful lump to her throat.

Dumb, Megan, she told herself. Really dumb. You're going to let that good, solid brick wall you've built around yourself crumble because the guy sleeps in a room with wallpaper and a pineapple bedstead.

Kitchen sounds drifted up to her. The refrigerator opened and closed, spoons clanked on glass bowls, and there was a soft splat followed by an expletive. "What happened?" she called down.

"I dropped a damn egg on the damn floor, and all the king's horses and all the king's men can't put Humpty-Dumpty together again. I wish you'd get down here. I have something to ask you."

She put her jeans back on and helped herself to a blue plaid flannel shirt hanging in Pat's closet. It all felt very intimate, wearing his shirt, using his shower. Downstairs their baby would sleep in his crib by the fireplace. And Pat was making domestic sounds in the kitchen, waiting to ask her something. Lord, what could it be? The Big Question? He'd already told her he wanted her. It was all a little sudden, but sometimes love was like that. Mr. and Mrs. Hunter. Megan Hunter. She looked at herself in the mirror. She was over the edge.

"Are you around the bend?" she asked her reflection. "Mrs. Hunter? Don't you ever learn?" She stomped down the stairs. "Just because I'm wearing your shirt, don't think I'm going to marry you."

He stared at her, blank-faced.

"Wasn't that what you were going to ask me?"

"No. I was going to ask you to crack the eggs for the gingerbread. I keep making a mess of it."

She looked at the brown dough in the big bowl on the counter. "Sure, I get all the tough jobs."

"So why don't you want to marry me?"

"Nothing personal. I don't want to marry anyone. I'm a free spirit. I'm the wind. I'm a saucy strumpet."

He grinned. "Do you know what a strumpet is?"

"Not exactly."

He whispered the definition in her ear.

"Hmmm," she said. "Well, I'm not one of those."

He draped his arm around her shoulders. "What about it, Windy? Will you crack my eggs?"

"I suppose it's the least I could do, since you've mixed everything else together."

An hour later, Megan took the last cookie sheet out of the oven and set it on a wire rack. "This isn't going to work," she told Pat. "You've already eaten half of the cookies. We'll never get enough for Thanksgiving at this rate."

"I can't help it. They're great. Besides, I'm not the only guilty party."

She planted her fists on her hips. "I ate one cookie. One!"

"Yes, but you're wearing half a dozen."

She examined her shirt. It was caked with cookie dough and smudged with flour. "I'm not a neat cook."

He tweaked her nose. "You're an adorable cook."

So they were back to nose tweaks, she thought, pouting. Fine. "I'm going home."

He looked disappointed. "I'll make cocoa and popcorn if you'll stay awhile longer."

69

"I can't. Tomorrow is Saturday. I have to work tomorrow." That much was true, but she could have stayed. She was just in a snit because he'd tweaked her on the nose. Men were so fickle. One minute they were slobbering all over you in a fit of passion, and the next thing they didn't want to marry you. The hell with them.

"Where's your car?" he asked. "I didn't see it when I parked in the garage."

"It's at Merchants Square. I went to see Tilly's apartment."

"She's not home." He plunged his hands into his pockets. "I check on her every day."

Megan glanced over at the little boy sleeping by the fireplace. "What happens if Tilly doesn't come back?"

Pat leaned against the wall and closed his eyes. "I don't know. I'd adopt him, honest to goodness I would, but it's not that easy. I'm not sure of the law. I think he'll be made a ward of the state, probably placed in a registered foster home until relatives can be located. Even if I tried to adopt him, it would take a year for the paper work to be done, and I probably wouldn't get him, because I'm not married."

"Isn't there anything we can do?"

Pat gritted his teeth when he saw the tears clinging to her lower lashes. He was close to tears himself, and he was mad. Tilly Coogan had disappointed him. She was a young unwed mother, but she'd seemed responsible and mature for her years. Timmy was a healthy, happy, well-loved baby. Ten days earlier Tilly and Timmy had left his office as a functioning family unit. And now she'd abandoned him. What had gone wrong? Maybe he should have been more observant. Maybe he could have prevented this.

He pulled Megan to him and hugged her, burying his face in her hair. "I don't know, Meg. I'm giving her until Thanksgiving, and then I'll hire a lawyer and a detective. In the meantime, we'll take good care of Timmy."

Megan blinked back the tears. "It's his first Thanksgiving. We have to do this right."

Pat smiled. "Yeah. He probably can't wait to sneeze turkey on you."

She slipped her arms into her pea coat. "I'll leave on that happy note."

Pat handed her the keys to his car. "How about if we swap cars for tonight? I don't want you wandering the streets alone."

He walked to the car with her and waited while it churned a few times and caught. "I'll come pick it up tomorrow at six o'clock. Wear something pretty. I'm taking you out to dinner. I think we both need a decent meal."

"What about Timmy?"

"I have a baby-sitter. My receptionist's daughter."

The following day, Saturday, Megan dressed in her colonial costume, skipped down the stairs of her house, locked her front door with a flourish, and whistled all the way to work. She cracked her knuckles throughout the day, glancing at the watch she had hidden in her pocket, sighing heavily when time seemed to drag. At five o'clock she bolted from her ticket-taking post in front of the silversmith's shop, and at five-thirty she flew into her house and practically jumped out of her big, black shoes. She dropped her long skirt and white apron at the top of the stairs and was stripped down to her long johns by the time she reached the bathroom.

She had a dinner date with Patrick Hunter, and she only had half an hour to make herself ravishing. She caught a glimpse of her red cheeks and flyaway hair in the vanity mirror. Maybe not ravishing, she thought. Ravishing would take days. In thirty minutes the most she could accomplish would be to look clean and presentable.

Half an hour later, Megan applied the final swipe of mascara to her lashes and stepped back to appraise herself. She wasn't sure how she looked, but she *felt* ravishing. She'd used the blow dryer and brush on her hair until it was a shining cloud of soft waves around her face. She wore a smudge of eye liner, a little peach-toned blush over cheeks that were already flushed, and a pale coral lip gloss.

"Geez," she murmured, "is that me? Last time I got dressed up like this was in April . . . for my wedding."

Pat knocked once and let himself into the house. He wasn't sure what he'd expected. A khaki jumper or a denim skirt. Maybe a pair of dressy corduroy slacks. He was completely unprepared for the woman who appeared at the top of the stairs.

She could have stepped off the cover of a magazine or hosted an exclusive Washington tea. She wore a pale pink sweater and matching skirt. The outfit was belted at her waist and clung to all her delicious curves and made her hair seem impossibly red. The slim skirt came to just above her knee, baring long, shapely legs in silky tinted stockings. Her dressy heels matched her small black handbag.

"I can't believe I made it on time!" she said breathlessly.

He nodded. He didn't know what to say. Megan Murphy was so many different people, he couldn't keep up with them all. He watched her hair swing around her shoulders as she descended the stairs, and wasn't sure how he would get through the evening. She was breathtaking . . . and he was just a cute pediatrician.

"Are you Megan Murphy?" he asked. He wanted to make sure. "You're beautiful." He reached out to touch her sleeve. "What's this soft, fuzzy stuff?"

"It's an angora blend. Do you like it?"

Like it? He wanted to get naked on it. Good thing they had a six-thirty reservation and had to leave the house immediately. He was afraid once he started fondling Megan Murphy in her bunny dress, he'd lose control.

It wasn't in the plan for him to lose control. This was their first date. It was supposed to be romantic and civilized. Extreme fondling on a first date wasn't civilized, he told himself, helping her with her black wool coat.

He locked the house and held the driver's door open for her. "The other door is broken," he explained, and immediately decided he would never get it fixed when he saw her dress ride high on her thigh as she slid across the seat.

He drove to the historic area and pulled into a parking lot on Francis Street. "I thought we'd eat at the King's Arms Tavern," he said. It had been the most romantic, elegant restaurant he could imagine, but suddenly he worried that this exquisite creature sitting next to him might be jaded. Surely she was taken to expensive restaurants every day of the week and had eaten at the King's Arms hundreds of times.

Her eyes brightened. "I've never eaten here," she said excitedly. "I could never afford it. I've been to Christiana Campbell's for lunch, but never the King's Arms."

She slipped her hand into his as they crossed the street and walked through the dark garden

75

behind the tavern. "Do you know what they serve here? Colonial game pie and fig ice cream and oyster pie. I have the menu memorized!"

He couldn't believe it. She'd never eaten at the King's Arms. He knew she didn't want to get married, but didn't she even date?

The garden led to an alley that led to Duke of Gloucester Street. The street was nearly empty, with only a few people strolling toward the King's Arms. Candles flickered in the wavy-glass tavern windows. Megan and Pat read the bill of fare while they waited to be called inside.

"They have wandering musicians here," Megan said, "and everything's lit by candles. And the waiters wear knee breeches. You probably know all that." She smiled, slightly embarrassed at her enthusiasm.

"Nope. I'm new in town, and it's nice to have my very own tour guide."

"I guess I'm new too. I moved to Williamsburg in June. I needed to get away from . . . things. I really love it here. I've always been a history buff."

They stepped into the tavern and were seated at a small table by a fireplace. A candle flickered in its glass chimney, illuminating the white linen tablecloth and formal place setting.

"I'm a history buff of sorts," Pat said. "My ancestors lived in Williamsburg when Lord Botetourt served as governor. I was born and raised in California, but I've always been drawn to Williamsburg. Now that I'm here, I feel like I've come home."

Megan nodded. She knew exactly what he meant. She didn't have Williamsburg roots, but her heart told her this was where she belonged.

She gave the costumed waiter her order and her menu and watched Pat. She liked the way he looked in the candlelight. It made his eyes dark and mysterious, and emphasized the few laugh lines around them. He was wearing a navy blazer, navy stripped tie, and a white shirt with a small blue check pattern.

When their soup arrived, he regarded his bowl with undisguised apprehension. "You ever have peanut soup before?" he asked.

"It's supposed to be good." She delicately stirred the muddy brown concoction in front of her. She sniffed at it, then dipped a small chunk of toast called a sippet into the soup.

"Well?" he asked.

She thoughtfully chewed her soup-coated sippet. "I like it. You can try yours now, you coward. Where's your sense of adventure?"

He grinned. "I leave adventure up to you. I'm the laid-back, sensible country doctor."

Sometimes, she thought. He definitely had an easygoing California style, but there was nothing laid back about his kisses. And he was slightly crazy. Not an out-of-control craziness. Pat had a quiet, teasing sense of humor that was often turned inward. Her initial impression of him had been wrong, she admitted. He was responsible, sensitive, mature, and very caring. It was his self-confidence and the fact that he liked himself and the world around him that allowed him to be a little crazy.

She made several selections from the relish tray offered to her and smiled at Pat. "I've been thinking that you're a little crazy."

He seemed surprised at that. "Me? Dull Pat?"

She tasted the sweet corn. "You're the only person I know who has a rabbit hopping around in his house. And you have an . . . um, unusual sense of humor."

The waiter returned with warm Sally Lunn bread and tiny Indian corn muffins. Pat made a small mountain of muffins on his bread plate. "My sense of humor has always gotten me in trouble. My first year in med school I got Jimmy Szlagy to help me steal a cadaver and—" He stopped abruptly and grimaced. "You probably don't want to hear about this while we're eating."

She scraped the final dregs of soup onto the last chunk of toast. "I probably don't." She slathered butter on a thick wedge of bread and closed her eyes in epicurean anticipation. "Yum."

Pat relaxed back in his chair and watched her. She was a person filled to the brim with a love of life, he thought. Eating wasn't a bodily function to her. It was a celebration. "You're the only woman I've ever dated who got orgasmic over bread," he said huskily, then smiled. "Are you as easily pleased in bed as you are at the dinner table?"

Megan paused with her slice of bread midway to her mouth. A thrill raced through her when she realized she'd been waiting for this. She wanted him to flirt with her. She might even want to be seduced. Her gaze caught and held his as she tested the texture of the bread with the tip of her tongue. She sensually licked a buttery fingertip, enjoying his rapt attention, and lowered her lashes. "There are some things a man should find out for himself."

He raised his eyebrows. "Is that an invitation?"

She tipped her head back and laughed softly. It was fun being a temptress in a crowded restaurant, she thought. It was exciting and relatively safe. She paused while the waiter replaced her soup bowl with a salad dish.

"It's an opinion," she said, spearing a tomato with her fork, "and I think I've been saved by the salad."

Pat wagged a finger at her. "Nothing can save you, Megan Murphy. Destiny has brought us together. It's been predetermined that your beautiful, silky red hair should be spread across my pillow."

"Destiny had nothing to do with it," she said, suddenly nervous, not sure if she should let the conversation continue in this direction. "It was your adventurous rabbit that brought us together."

A minstrel wandered into the candlelit room, playing an eighteenth-century ballad on his guitar. Megan turned to face him, but thoughts of Pat and his pillow were spinning in her head. The minstrel's tunes, the elegant table, the room filled with people intermingled in a kaleidoscope of sights and sounds that were soft-edged in comparison to the clarity of her desire. She wanted to sleep with Patrick Hunter. She wanted to know him in the most intimate way possible.

She busied herself with her main course, spreading a bit of currant jelly across the flaky brown crust of the game pie, as her waiter had suggested. She mechanically tasted slivers of duck, rabbit, and venison, and was surprised when her plate was empty. "I ate all that?"

Pat sipped his wine. "You seemed preoccupied."

Preoccupied, she thought. If he only knew. She'd spend the entire meal mentally making love to him.

They finished the meal with raisin rice pudding and coffee. "I can't eat another bite," Megan said. "In fact, I may never eat again."

Pat helped her into her coat. "Now for the

really exciting part of the evening. I'm going to take you to the movies." He slung his arm around her shoulders and hurried her through the garden to the parking lot. "My parents have taken pity on their poor, deprived son and sent him a TV and a DVD player."

"How nice!"

"I have great parents. I can't wait for you to meet them. I'm glad they're coming here for Thanksgiving."

"I have great parents too. Thank goodness they're in Florida."

He started the engine and looked at her sideways. "What's wrong with them?"

"Nothing. The problem is, they have this super marriage. And since this marriage has made them so happy, they want me to have a super marriage too."

"And you don't want to get married."

She stared straight ahead as they drove along Waller Street. "Right."

She wasn't sure anymore, though. Two weeks ago she'd been comfortably on her way to spinsterhood. Now she was caught in the middle of a ready-made family, and she liked it. At the end of the week, she'd woken up before the alarm rang, eager to see Timmy and Pat. And this morning she'd caught herself brooding because she hadn't awakened in the cozy pineapple four-poster on Nicholson Street. Awakening in Pat's bed was a dangerous daydream. Her emotions weren't listening to reason.

It was an interesting phenomenon, she mused. She suspected that in other relationships she'd followed reason and tried to fabricate emotions. This time her emotions were running amuck, and at the head of the list was passion.

She studied Pat's dark, boyish profile and wondered if she could indulge herself. Her body answered immediately *Yes!* Her mind worked more slowly. It said maybe.

Chapter 5

Megan made a fire while Pat took the baby-sitter home. There weren't many places to hide a television and a DVD player in the little cottage, she thought. Obviously, they weren't downstairs. That left the bedroom.

She tucked a blanket around Timmy and turned toward the stairs. Stiffening her back, she took a few steps forward. So what if the television was in his bedroom? she asked herself. It was the logical place. Outdoor antennas weren't allowed in the historic area, so it made sense to have the television on the second floor, where it would get better reception. Besides, Timmy was downstairs. The noise might wake him. Yup, it was only logical to put the television in the bedroom. And it was only logical to sit on the big four-poster to watch the movie, she thought as she climbed the stairs.

Well, there they were. A brand-new TV and a brand-new DVD player. She stood in front of them, chewing on her lower lip and wondering what movie he'd gotten. If it was rated X she was going to jump out the window. She was definitely physically ready to share a bed with Pat, but her mind was still stuck on maybe. And there was this other emotion crowding onto the scene. Panic.

When Pat walked into the room a few minutes later he speculated on Megan's mood. She was nervous. She'd enjoyed the flirting at the restaurant, but only to a point. Then she'd tuned him out. She was making up her mind, he decided. She was attracted to him, but she was afraid. His instincts told him to go slowly. He'd waited thirty years for her. He could wait a little longer to make things exactly right.

He took a plastic bag from the dresser. "I got *Winnie the Pooh and the Blustery Day*. It's my favorite. And I got *Bridges of Madison County*. I missed it when it came out."

"*Winnie the Pooh?*"

"For Timmy."

She noticed a tag taped to the top of the DVD player. "Happy Birthday from Mom and Dad," she read. "It's your birthday? Why didn't you tell me?"

"I'd honestly forgotten about it until the DVD player and the TV arrived this morning. This has been a busy week for me. I'm not used to being a daddy."

"Happy birthday."

"Thanks." He popped *Winnie the Pooh* into the recorder slot and zapped it with the remote.

"I thought *Winnie* was for Timmy."

Pat grinned. "We should check it out. Make sure everythings okay. I wouldn't want the little nipper to be disappointed."

Megan stepped out of her shoes and climbed onto the soft feather quilt. She plumped a pillow at the headboard and curled her legs under her. "This is cozy. It's a perfect night for *Winnie the Pooh.*"

Pat looked at the woman sitting on his bed and felt his mouth go dry. She was exquisite, and somehow, watching her take off her shoes had been as erotic as if she'd been taking off her panties. Lord, he must have been crazy.

How would he ever get through the evening without attacking her?

Megan felt the tension creeping through her body. She leaned back against the pillow and willed herself to relax. She wanted to act like an adult and let this desire grow naturally. There was a right time for everything . . . a time to watch a movie, a time for conversation, a time to be kissed. She took a deep breath, carefully folded her hands in her lap, and watched the wind blow Owl's house down. Then she watched the windy day turn into a rainy night. She thought it must be nice to spend a rainy night in Patrick's bedroom. Good thing it wasn't raining. She might be tempted to set up housekeeping.

"Is this your furniture?" she asked to get her mind off the idea of living with Pat.

"No. My Aunt Catherine lives here. She's a historical interpreter, but she's taken a six-month leave to participate in an archeological dig somewhere. I'll have to find another house in March."

He changed movies and returned to the bed, putting his arm around Megan and snuggling her next to him. "This is a terrific way to spend a birthday," he murmured, kissing her hair. "Have you seen this movie?"

She closed her eyes for a moment, savoring the stab of pleasure his kiss had brought. "Six times, and I always cry. You'd better have lots of tissues handy."

Later, Megan dabbed at her red-rimmed eyes and blew her nose. "It's *so* beautiful," she said, gasping.

Pat held her close and stroked a stray strand of hair from her tear-streaked face. "Are you okay? I've never seen anyone cry like that over a movie. I never would have gotten it if I'd known what it did to you."

"No, I love it. It's my favorite movie."

"Honey, you started crying when they played the opening theme, and you absolutely sobbed through the whole last half hour!"

Megan snuffled against his chest. He was nice to cry on, she thought. Warm and strong and oozing security. This was much better than crying alone.

"I'm better now," she said, tipping her head up toward him. She was all cried out, and she wanted to be kissed. She liked Patrick Hunter. *Really* liked him. He was fun, and he was comfortable. And he was sexy. Very sexy. She hadn't changed her mind about marriage, but she thought a birthday kiss would be nice. Everyone needed to get kissed once in a while, and the "maybe" in her mind had changed to "probably."

"Happy birthday," she said in a voice husky from crying. She wound her arms around his neck and ran her finger along the outer rim of his ear.

Pat felt himself stir at her touch. He'd never wanted anything in his entire life the way he wanted Megan Murphy. He'd wanted her since the first moment he saw her, and that want had grown into a physical and emotional ache that nagged at him day and night. Now that he had her on his bed, waiting to be kissed, he was apprehensive. He didn't want her seduced into his arms by Clint Eastwood, and he didn't want her softened up by Winnie the Pooh or the fact that it was his birthday. He wanted her to want *him*, Patrick Hunter. He let his hands caress the pink angora sweater and felt the warm woman beneath.

"Meg, if we stay here, like this, I'm going to kiss you, and I'm not going to want to stop kissing you. Maybe I should take you home now."

Had he just offered to take her home? he wondered. He must be nuts. He finally had Megan right where he wanted her, and he'd offered to take her home.

"I don't want to go home," she said. "I want to be kissed."

Hell, he thought, that's the ball game. He'd reached the end of his altruism. Besides, she'd be insulted if he refused to kiss her, and it would be rude to insult her. He'd warned her about kissing's leading to other things, right? He'd told her in the beginning of the week that he'd do anything to get her. That put him in the clear, didn't it?

Megan watched emotions parade across Pat's face. Just when she wanted to get kissed he was going virtuous on her, she thought, waging some sort of war between his morals and his mattress. Wasn't that her luck? "Hunter?"

"Yes?"

"Stop thinking and kiss me."

A small frown appeared between his eyes as he lowered his head to hers. He kissed her gently, tasting, testing soft lips. "Megan, I don't—"

She stopped his words with a kiss of her own, leaning into him, pressing against his chest, sliding her stockinged legs along his. She closed her eyes and reveled in the warmth of his body. Desire raged through her, just as she'd known it would. This was a special night, she told herself. A stolen moment of love. She wasn't meant to be married, but she could have this one night.

Pat pulled her even closer. Megan gasped at the sudden intensity of his passion and arched up against him in a haze of greedy pleasure. Her fingers flew along the buttons of his shirt, baring his muscled chest to her touch. She wanted more. She wanted to see all of him. He pulled her sweater over her head and stripped off her bra.

"Pat . . ."

He looked at her with eyes black from desire. "Megan . . ."

"The baby's crying."

"What?"

"The baby's crying!"

"Oh, hell. I don't believe this. Let him cry." He kissed her hard on the mouth. Halfway through the kiss he opened his eyes and found her staring at him.

"I'm sorry," she said, practically screaming in exasperation. "I can't concentrate."

Pat counted to ten, took a deep breath, and heaved himself off the bed. "Feel free to continue without me. I have a feeling this is going to take some time."

Megan rolled her eyes. So this was motherhood, she thought. Green beans on your shirt and romantic interruptions. She pulled on her sweater, tidied her clothes and ran Pat's hairbrush through her tangled hair.

"What's the problem?" she asked, tiptoeing down the stairs.

Pat was cradling Timmy in his arms. "I think he's getting a tooth."

"Couldn't he get it during the day? Couldn't he get it tomorrow?"

Pat grinned. "Disappointed, huh? You're pretty hot stuff."

She felt her face flush.

"And you're fun to tease," he added, smiling. "How about some cold apple juice for Timmy and some hot chocolate for Pat?"

She clicked her heels together and gave him a snappy salute. "Aye, aye, sir."

They sat at the kitchen table, drinking their hot chocolate while Pat fed the baby.

"It's gone, isn't it?" he said to her.

She nodded. Yes, the moment was gone. Probably it was all for the best, she told herself. She needed time to think. She needed to be sure she could handle a physical relationship with Pat. She didn't believe in sex without commitment, but commitment didn't have to mean marriage. Could there be such a thing as temporary commitment? Limited commitment? Certainly there was more involved here than simple sex. If she made love with Pat would she be strong enough to pick up the pieces when the relationship ended? It was this last thought that worried her the most.

He touched her hand. "Are you still sorry Timmy stopped us?"

She smiled. "I don't know."

An honest answer, he thought. It wouldn't have been his.

She finished her cocoa and searched for her coat. "I think it's time I went home."

"Would you consider spending the night here?"

She let the idea roll through her mind, then sighed heavily. "No. I'd consider the loan of your car, though. I'll drop it off on my way to work tomorrow morning."

The next day Megan stood in the doorway of the cooper's shop at the west end of Duke of Gloucester Street, just across from Bruton Parish Church. The air was sweet with the smell of shaved wood, a nippy breeze played in the bare tree limbs, and the tower bells pealed noontime in Bruton Parish. She watched Pat and Timmy cross the street and follow a tour group to her station. After checking everyone's ticket, she turned to Pat and grimaced at the dark circles under his bloodshot eyes. "You look awful."

"I didn't sleep all night. From now on I'm going to be more sympathetic to the parents of teething babies."

Timmy was slouched in the stroller, sound asleep.

"You sure you're not hallucinating?" she asked. "This kid's out like a light."

"This is the only time he sleeps. He wakes up the minute I get him in the house. I've been pushing him around for hours. Seems like days."

"I wish I could help you, but I don't get off work until five."

"I'll be dead by five."

She smiled. "Try to survive. We're scheduled to make red cabbage and cranberry sauce tonight."

"Don't those things come in jars?"

Her eyes widened. "What about our old-fashioned Thanksgiving?"

"Maybe we should modernize it. I could cook some burgers on the barbecue and buy a bunch of pies at the supermarket. If I wait until Thursday, they'll be on sale."

"I'm going to pretend I didn't hear any of this."

"Megan Murphy, you're a hard woman." His gaze dropped to her chest. "Fortunately, even though you're a hard woman, you still have a few soft spots."

"I thought you were supposed to be tired."

"I'm beginning to wake up." His voice grew husky. "We have unfinished business."

"I think so too."

Pat's mouth dropped open.

"After all, I'm twenty-seven years old, and I have normal biological urges and emotional needs. Just because I'm destined never to get married doesn't mean I can't ... um, get debauched."

"I wish I weren't so tired. Now I'm starting to imagine things. Did you just say you wanted to get debauched?"

"Yes. The sooner the better. How about right after the red cabbage? It has to cook for three hours, anyway. It would give us something to do."

At five o'clock Timmy was sitting in his high chair, gnawing on his drool-soaked blanket while Pat called out for a pizza.

"Listen kid," Pat said, returning to the table, "you've got to help me out here. I've got a long night ahead of me. I've got to debauch Megan for three hours. I'm gonna need some quiet." He was going to need more than quiet, he thought. He was going to need a transfusion. He was out on his feet.

Timmy blinked and pounded his tray table. His face turned red and crinkled, and he began to whimper. "Mum, mum, mum," he cried.

"Poor kid." Pat lifted Timmy out of the chair.

"Teething and no mum, mum, mum to comfort you."

Even if Mum returned, Pat wasn't so sure he wanted to entrust Timmy to her care. Not even a phone call all this time she'd been gone. Not even a letter. Not his idea of a loving mother.

Megan and the pizza delivery boy arrived at Pat's house simultaneously.

"Deliveries for Patrick Hunter," she announced. "One pizza and a strumpet to go."

"Hear that, Tim. They sent us a strumpet with our pizza. What do you suppose we should do with it?" Pat paid for the pizza and handed Timmy over to Megan. "Timmy says we should have the strumpet for dessert. What do you think?"

"I think I'll take a shower."

"I'll put the pizza away. We can eat it tomorrow."

"Fine with me," Megan commented as she sashayed from the room.

When Megan got out of the shower she found the bedroom candles lit and the comforter turned down. The stairs creaked, and Pat walked into the room, carrying two crystal brandy snifters.

"Timmy's asleep," he said. "The tooth has broken through the gum. I think he'll be okay now."

He handed her a glass. "I've warmed some brandy for us." He took a sip from his own glass and set it on the night table. "Are you sure, Meg?"

Megan just looked at him. How could you ever be sure? she wondered. She'd thought she was sure with David. Look where that had gotten her. No guarantees, she told herself, but this felt right. She liked and respected Pat . . . and she might as well admit it, she'd fallen for him. She didn't want to run away.

The night before, she'd stood looking at the plastic bag hanging in her closet. She'd broken out in a cold sweat at the memories it had provoked, but that hadn't changed her feelings for Pat. It would be terrible to ruin something beautiful and special because of that bag, she'd thought. She'd take a chance and go one step at a time.

"You have beets in your hair," she said. "Why don't you take a shower, and I'll get comfy." She waited until the bathroom door clicked closed, then dropped her towel and slid between the cool sheets. She tucked the comforter under her arms and listened to the water spraying against the stall door. It was a nice, intimate sound. A husbandly, loving sound.

The water stopped, and moments later Pat emerged, wearing a short royal-blue terrycloth robe. He sat on the edge of the bed and kissed her. "Mmmm," he said. "Brandy."

"I toasted you while you were in the bathroom."

"What did you say?"

"To Pat, the cute pediatrician."

He made a face. "That's not very romantic."

"Okay, then *you* do the toast."

He thought a moment. "To Tibbles, for bringing you to me."

"To Tibbles." She sighed and wrapped her arms around his neck, allowing the comforter to slip below her breasts.

His hands skimmed along her neck and her shoulders, and down her arms. She'd finally come to him, and he wanted to please her, protect her, comfort her, cuddle her. He was overwhelmed by the loving feelings flooding through him, barely able to breathe, wanting to cover her with kisses.

Megan writhed under his touch. She moaned and arched her back as his fingers caressed and explored.

Afterward she lay cradled in his arms, under the down comforter, watching the candles burn low in the pewter candlesticks. She hadn't made a mistake this time. This time everything was right. She belonged here, in his bed, in his arms. She smiled at his even breathing, delighting in the fact that he was asleep and she was awake. It gave her a chance to enjoy him in a more quiet, contemplative fashion. This was nice, she thought. Very, very nice.

Chapter 6

Megan lay still as a clam, barely breathing, contemplating the situation. It was official. She had a lover. She'd spent the night with Patrick Hunter. A ripple of excitement caused an involuntary shiver to rush through her. It was thrilling and scary and awkward. She'd been engaged twice before, but she had never felt the jumble of emotions that were flooding through her now. Her engagements had been sterile and orderly compared to this. And she'd never spent the night.

She was new to this morning-after stuff. What the devil was she supposed to do? She needed a cup of coffee, but her lover was still sound asleep. She had a brief thought of dallying with him in his sleep but dismissed it as unethical. She stretched luxuriously and glanced at the bedside clock. Seven-thirty. *Seven-thirty?* Pat was supposed to be at the hospital at six!

"Pat, wake up. It's seven-thirty."

"Mmmm."

She shook him gently. "You have to get up. You're late."

He sighed and rolled onto his stomach.

What did it take to get the man out of bed, a cattle prod? "Pat!"

He burrowed under his pillow.

Megan hopped up and tore the covers off him. She stood motionless for a moment in awed admiration. Lord, he was grogeous. But there was no time for ogling, she thought regretfully. He still wasn't moving.

"Pat, if you don't get up I'm going to do something drastic! *Pat!*" She wrapped herself in his robe and padded into the bathroom.

"Okay, you asked for it," she said, returning with a glass of cold water.

She stood poised over his naked body. Where should she spill it? He mumbled in his sleep and rolled onto his back, and Megan closed her eyes and dumped the water.

"Holy—!" he shouted, springing put of bed. "What the hell?"

"I couldn't get you to wake up. It's seven-thirty."

"Oh, no." He groaned. "How could I have slept so long?" He looked down at himself. "What happened?"

"I poured some water on you to wake you up."

His eyes were wide with incredulity, and his voice cracked. "I'm soaked!"

"It was sort of an accident."

He dashed for the bathroom. "Get me some orange juice. I'll be down in five minutes."

Megan slapped a lump of clay onto her potter's wheel. She looked at it reverently, imagining the teapot she was about to create, anticipating the sensuous feel of the clay whirling against her fingers.

Ever since she was a little girl she'd had a compulsion to make things. Paintings, poems, mittens, kites. She had a deep love of creation, of watching a blank canvas take on color and form, a length of yarn twist and knot into a knitted cap. When she went to the sea she made sand castles. When she was housebound by a snowstorm she made snowmen. When the wind whipped her hair across her face she made kites.

She didn't think of herself as an artist or craftswoman. She simply considered herself a maker of things. Now she knew how to make a pie, and it had given her almost as much pleasure as making a teapot.

She drizzled some water over the clay, pressed the foot pedal to turn the wheel, and applied firm pressure to the muddy-looking lump, centering it in the circle of her hands. The slick red-brown clay spun against her palms as she forced it into a conical shape. She pushed with her thumbs and returned it to a squat cylinder.

Megan loved working with clay. It was malleable and of the earth. It felt alive in her hands, and when she stopped the wheel and closed her eyes, she could still feel the warm clay moving across her fingertips.

She drew the clay up with steady hands, expertly shaping it into a globe, using her fingers to form a lip at the top. At last she stopped the wheel and examined her creation with a critical eye. "Pretty nice, huh?" she said to Timmy. He looked at her over the rim of his playpen, clapped his hands, and laughed.

It was warm in the outbuilding-turned-pottery-studio, thanks to an electric heater. Outside, a cold rain slathered down in sheets, thundering on the shingled roof, spattering against the two small windows. She started when the door suddenly flew open and Pat appeared. He closed the door, leaned against it, and dripped.

"Is it true turkeys are so stupid they'll stand out in the rain and drown?" he asked. "That's how I feel. Like a drowned turkey."

She rinsed the clay from her hands and wiped them on a paper towel. "How did you manage to get so wet? And what are you doing here? Is something wrong?"

"I decided to have lunch with you and Tim. As soon as I got on the road the drizzle turned into a downpour. Then I hit a pothole and the window on the driver's side went 'clink' and slid down into the door, never to be seen again. I had to drive all the way with the window down."

Rain dripped from bangs plastered to his forehead and ran in rivulets down his neck, soaking his shirt. His slacks were wet, though his shoes looked relatively dry. He rubbed his hands together to warm them. "And my heater doesn't work."

Megan couldn't help smiling. Patrick Hunter was especially huggable when he needed rescuing. She lifted Tim from the playpen and held him close while she draped an enormous army-surplus poncho over herself. She ducked under the hood and opened the door. "Come on, turkey, race you to the house."

Ten minutes later Pat sat at the kitchen table sipping hot coffee, wrapped in Megan's pink chenille robe while his clothes tumbled in the dryer. He wanted to pull Megan onto his lap and cuddle her, but she was busy opening a can of soup. Today was Tuesday. She'd shared his bed for two nights, and he was obsessed with her. He couldn't work. He couldn't eat. He could only remember, and the memories were keeping him in a constant state of euphoric arousal. He was hopelessly, totally, ridiculously in love, he thought. He couldn't tell if he was happily miserable or miserably happy. It was torture.

She refilled his coffee cup, and they both went still at the sound of a car pulling into the driveway. "Probably my neighbor," Megan said. "She keeps her horse here. Rents the barn and the pasture."

Two car doors slammed, followed by loud rapping at the front door. Megan answered the door and took a step backward. "Mom!"

The woman flung her arms around Megan and gave her a hug. "We couldn't stand Thanksgiving in Florida all by ourselves, so here we are! Surprise!"

"Surprise," Megan mumbled dumbly.

Her burly, red-haired father shoved two enormous suitcases through the door and shook the water off his plastic raincoat. "Good to see you, hon . . ." he began, but his voice trailed off as he stared beyond Megan, into the kitchen.

She turned her head and stared with him. "Oh, my God," she whispered at the sight of Pat, sitting at the kitchen table with hairy legs and hairy chest hanging out of the pink robe her parents had given her for Christmas. The picture was enhanced by the fact that he was wearing black dress socks and holding a baby.

"I can explain this," she said, watching her father's face turn brick red. Lord, she hoped he wasn't wearing his revolver.

Megan's mother started to giggle. She had her hand clapped over her mouth, but she was shaking with laughter. "I'm sorry," she said. "We should have phoned first."

"I don't see what's so damned funny," Megan's father roared.

"My word, Mike, the man's wearing black socks and Megan's robe. He looks silly."

"He looks *naked*! What the hell's going on around here?"

"It's all very simple," Megan said, following her father as he stalked into the kitchen. "Pat came over for lunch, and—"

Megan's mother took Timmy from Pat. "Megan, this is a baby."

"It's sort of Pat's."

Megan's father scowled at Pat. "I assume this is Pat?"

Pat stood and extended his hand. "Pat Hunter. Nice to meet you, sir."

"You always dress up in women's clothes?"

"Um, no, but it was cold sitting on the kitchen chair—"

"Are you married to my daughter?"

Pat shook his head. "She won't marry me."

"That does it!" Megan's father grabbed him

by a chenille lapel and punched him in the nose.

Pat tripped over his chair and sprawled onto the kitchen floor. He tenderly touched his bloody nose. "Oh, hell."

"Daddy!" Megan shouted. "How dare you! Criminy sakes, you can't just go around punching people out!" She rushed to Pat's side with a wet towel. "I'm sorry. Are you okay?"

"I think my nose is broken."

She glared at her father. "I hope you're satisfied."

"Actually, I feel a little foolish. I just hit a guy wearing a skirt."

"It's not a skirt. It's a robe," Pat said, getting to his feet. "And if it bothers you that much, I'll take the damn thing off."

Megan's mother screamed and closed her eyes.

Megan whistled through her teeth and raised her arms. "Stop! Daddy, you take the suitcases upstairs to the guest bedroom. Mom, please take care of Timmy until I get back. And you," she said to Pat, "you will get dressed, so I can drive you to the hospital to get your stupid nose X-rayed."

She stomped off to the laundry room and returned with Pat's clothes. "You can change in the downstairs bathroom," she told him.

Patrick Hunter and Mike Murphy stood toe to toe for a moment in silent, furious appraisal of each other.

Megan glared at both of them. "Daddy, the suitcases, *now!*" She sighed, and almost collapsed with relief when the two men turned from each other and went in opposite directions.

She dumped the contents of an ice tray into a plastic bag and crushed the ice with a rolling pin. "Well, Mom," she said, "what do you think of Pat?"

"Nice legs. Cute little nose. It's a shame it got broken."

Megan smiled at her mother. "It needed character."

"Do you love him?"

Oh, boy, here we go, Megan thought, dropping the poncho over her head. "Don't start asking questions, Mom. Don't hire a hall for the reception. Don't start planning a surprise shower. Don't contemplate names for your grandchildren. This man is a pediatrician, and—"

Mrs. Murphy's eyes lit up. "A doctor? How nice!"

Megan thunked her fist against her forehead. Try a different approach, she told herself. "I don't think Daddy likes him."

"Nonsense. Your father was just taken by surprise. He didn't expect to find a naked man in your kitchen."

Megan grabbed her car keys as Pat emerged from the bathroom. She handed him the ice bag and quickly ushered him past her mother. "Make yourself at home, Mom. Fix Daddy some lunch."

Pat slouched in the passenger seat, pressing the ice and a towel to his bloody nose. "Fix Daddy some lunch," he mumbled. "What does he eat, raw meat and Christians? He ever been accused of police brutality?"

"He's really very sweet. He just got excited."

"It's no wonder you're not married yet. The life expectancy of your boyfriends must be about two hours."

Megan pushed the poncho hood off and pulled out of the driveway, thinking she should be so lucky. Her parents had a knack for turning boyfriends into fiancés in an alarmingly short period of time. Unfortunately, their coercive talents stopped just short of the altar.

"My other boyfriends have never had to worry about life expectancy. They were smart enough to keep their clothes on in front of my father."

Pat scowled and sank deeper into his seat. He didn't like the idea of other boyfriends. He especially hated the idea of other boyfriends without clothes. He wasn't a violent person, but if he ever met any of those other boyfriends, he'd punch them in the nose.

Suddenly he liked Megan's father. Yessir, the man was okay. This was going to be a great Thanksgiving. His family. Her family. Megan. Timmy. "Do you think I should order a larger turkey?"

"I think you should order a smaller turkey, since I won't be there."

"Of course you'll be there. You and your mother and father."

Megan stared at him. "Are you crazy? I'm not putting you and my father in the same room."

Pat rearranged the ice bag. "Don't worry

about it. Your father and I will get along just fine."

That was exactly what she was worried about, Megan thought. She'd come to believe that having your parents' approval was like the kiss of death to a romance.

Megan brushed her hair behind her ears and returned to her apple peeling. Nothing in her twenty-seven years of life as an only child had prepared her for this day. There were seven women and three children packed into the tiny cottage, all in the throes of preparing the next day's Thanksgiving feast. Timmy sat in his crib by the fireplace, sucking his thumb with a vengeance and watching the activity. Pat's four-year-old niece and six-year-old nephew were making hand-shaped cookies out of leftover pie crust. Mrs. Hunter and Mrs. Murphy presided over a mammoth bowl of stuffing.

"A little sage," Mrs. Murphy said, "and more sausage."

"And apples," Mrs. Hunter said. "Needs apples."

Megan's mother dropped a handful of sliced

apples into the bowl. "So when do you think they should get married?"

Mrs. Hunter thoughtfully tasted a lump of raw stuffing. "A spring wedding would be nice, but they have the child. . . ."

Both women turned and looked at Timmy.

"Christmas," Mrs. Murphy said. "It would be best to marry as soon as possible. It would look better for the adoption."

Megan ground her teeth and bent over the bowl of sliced apples.

Pat's sister Laurie was sitting across from Megan. She leaned over and whispered, "Your mom and my mom sure hit it off."

Megan made a strangled sound in her throat.

"I think they're planning your wedding."

"They're in for a big surprise. I'm *not* getting married."

"What about Timmy? Don't you have to get married before you can adopt Timmy?"

Megan stared at the pile of apple peelings. Everyone assumed Timmy's mother wouldn't return, especially since they hadn't heard from her in all the time she'd been gone. Megan couldn't remember what her life had been like before Timmy. And it was true: If Pat didn't have a wife, he wouldn't stand a chance of adopting the baby. Not a good reason to get married, she thought. You were supposed to get married because you were in love. Megan, her inner voice whispered, you *are* in love.

"So when do you think you'll get married?" Laurie asked.

"Christmas," Megan said. "A Christmas wedding in Williamsburg."

The front door was flung open, filling the cottage with a welcome blast of cold air. Pat and his brother staggered in under a load of boxes and bags.

"Here it is!" Pat announced. His cheeks were flushed, his jaunty red scarf askew, and he was laughing as he set an enormous cardboard carton on the table.

Everyone crowded around to look into the box.

"What is it?" Megan's mother asked.

"It's the turkey!" Pat said.

"Turkeys don't come that big," Mrs. Murphy said. "It must be an ostrich."

Mrs. Hunter shook her head. "You'd better measure it. I don't think it'll fit in the oven."

Mrs. Murphy held her big wooden spoon aloft. "We need more stuffing."

"We need more people," Mrs. Hunter said. "This bird could feed the Pacific fleet."

Pat beamed. "It's a beauty, isn't it?"

Hours later Megan was sprawled on the braided rug, toasting her stockinged feet by the heat of the fire. "I don't ever want to see another apple," she said to Pat. "Look at my finger. It's got a blister from paring."

He looked solicitous and kissed the injured finger.

His niece giggled. "Pat kissed Megan's finger," she said.

"It's all right," Mrs. Murphy said. "They're going to get married. You can do that sort of thing when you're engaged to get married."

Pat leaned close to Megan and whispered in her ear. "Did I miss something? Are we engaged?"

"Yup. Your mom and my mom decided it this afternoon."

"Have they decided on a date?"

"Christmas."

Pat considered it for a moment. "You seem pretty mellow about all this."

"I'm trying to keep a sense of humor. Besides, my jaw aches from grinding my teeth."

He stretched out on his back beside her and clasped his hands behind his head. "Are you going to do it?"

"Do what?"

He grinned. "Marry me."

"I don't know. Do you think I should?"

"It's the least you could do after having your way with me two nights in a row. And it would probably help my tax return. Of course, it would ruin my image as a cute bachelor."

She looked at his nose. It wasn't broken, and the swelling was going down, but he was left with a classic shiner. "I think your image might be a little tarnished anyway."

Mrs. Hunter finished feeding Timmy and sat with him in the rocking chair. "Don't you think Timmy resembles Pat?" she asked Megan's mother. "Around the mouth?"

"Maybe, but he has Megan's eyes."

Megan groaned. "Mom, he doesn't have my

eyes. He has Tilly Coogan's eyes. This is Tilly Coogan's baby."

"I know that, dear. But there is a little resemblance growing here. You remember Mrs. Yates and her poodle, and how they looked like each other? And what about Skokey Moyer and that old bloodhound he kept?"

"I think they've gone off the deep end," Megan said to Pat.

He agreed. "Jumped in with both feet." There was a moment of silence. "Still, you have to admit, he does sort of have my mouth."

"I think that punch in the nose went straight to your brain."

"Nope. It's you. You make me starry-eyed and fuzzy-headed, and all warm and mushy inside."

"Yuk."

His eyes grew serious. He lowered his voice, so only she could hear. "It's true. I can't concentrate on anything. My stomach's a mess. My libido's out of control. Meg, I'm so in love with you it hurts. I can't stand being away from you, and when I'm with you I can't stand not touching you, holding you."

Megan felt her stomach flip and press against

her backbone. She experienced the same pain of separation, the same overwhelming desire to join flesh to flesh. For once, she couldn't blame her mother for jumping to conclusions. Any emotion this strong had to be obvious even to the most casual observer.

She touched her fingertip to his lips, and they exchanged smiles, acknowledging the mysterious power their love held over them.

There was the scrape of a kitchen chair as Mr. Murphy stood and stretched. "I think it's time to call it a night. I've had my supper, lost two games of chess, and need to soak my hand in hot water and Epsom salts." He tenderly rubbed his swollen, bruised knuckles. "Patrick, you've got a hard nose."

Everyone laughed. The story had already grown to classic proportions and was guaranteed immortality in both families.

"Patrick Hunter is a nice young man," Megan's father said as he drove them home in his rental car.

"A doctor," her mother added. "And his family is wonderful."

"I like him," Mr. Murphy said. "I even like him better than David."

Mrs. Murphy clapped her hand to her forehead. "Oh, dear! David!"

Megan leaned forward from the back seat. "What do you mean, 'Oh, dear, David'? What about David?"

Mrs. Murphy waved the issue away. "Nothing. Nothing to worry about."

"Then why am I worrying?" Megan asked. "Why do I have this awful feeling in the pit of my stomach?"

Mrs. Murphy glanced back at her daughter. "It's just that David called last week. He was wondering about you."

"And?"

"And he wanted to know where you were living. Well, heavens, Megan, you never tell us anything. We didn't know you had a new boyfriend."

Megan closed her eyes. "He isn't coming here."

"He is. He's stopping around after Thanksgiving."

"I'm going to slash my wrists."

"I think he's still interested in you. He mentioned something about reconsidering."

"What?" Megan yelled. "That toad. That slime ball. I'll reconsider him to the moon."

She sat back with a sigh. In all honesty, she didn't know why she was so mad. David had done her a favor. She'd never truly been in love with him. She realized that now. When the chips were down, he'd been the one with the guts. She'd stood quaking in her fancy shoes, afraid to admit she'd made a horrible mistake, and David had been the one to say "no." At the time it hadn't seemed like a kindness. At the time it had been damned embarrassing.

"How come I never get to dump on anyone?" she mumbled. "How come I'm always the dumpee?"

Her mother smiled. "Maybe this is your chance, Megan. Maybe you'll get to dump on David. Wouldn't that be fun?"

Megan threw her head back and laughed out loud. Her mother might be a little pushy when it came to marriage, but she was a lesson in flexibility and finding the silver lining.

Chapter 7

Megan awoke before the alarm. She threw back the covers and dashed from her warm bed to see the sun rise through the frosty windowpane. It was Thanksgiving, and she couldn't have been more excited if it were Christmas and she were seven years old.

She stuffed her feet into a pair of warm socks and pulled on her jeans and sweat shirt. She'd planned to spend a few hours working in her studio that morning as a special treat to herself. She was going to make Christmas presents. A teapot for Pat and a bowl for Timmy.

She quietly closed the front door and crept across the frozen lawn, her breath making clouds in the crisp air. She switched the lights on in her studio and started the electric heater. Then she stood for a moment, warming her hands on the mug of hot coffee she'd brought from the kitchen, watching the steam rise from the black liquid, filling her head with the smell of morning.

She couldn't ever remember feeling more loved. She'd had a wonderful childhood, but she'd come to realize there were many kinds of love. The love one felt for parents, the love a woman shared with a man, the love a mother felt for her child. She had to smile at herself. She felt swollen . . . no, downright bloated with happiness.

She slipped a mud-spattered lab coat on and prepared her clay, whistling as she worked, focusing her attention on her craft. By nine-thirty she had her projects drying on a board and was ready for another cup of coffee.

Pat met her halfway to the house. "I'm done with my rounds at the hospital and need a kiss," he said. He swept her into his arms and kissed her long and hard. "I've been feeling deprived since all these relatives descended on us. I miss waking up next to you."

"If my mother has her way, you'll wake up next to me for the rest of your life."

He nibbled on her neck. "Yum. Sounds nice."

"Hmmm." If it sounded so nice, Megan thought, why hadn't he asked her to marry him? Pat had taken all the talk of engagement and marriage in stride. He looked and sounded like a fiancé. But he had never seriously proposed, and the vagueness of their relationship nagged at her.

She didn't want to confront him with it, though. She wasn't sure what her answer would be if he asked. There was still a small corner of her that harbored misgivings about marriage. It wasn't so much *being* married that bothered Megan. It was the *getting* married that sent her heart into a nose dive.

Pat held her at arm's length and studied her face. It was unreadable. As unreadable as her "hmmm." He always sensed some reserve in Megan. It seemed alien to her character, but there it was. Always a "hmmm." He wasn't sure if it was a question or a statement, or maybe just a device to deter the natural progression of a conversation. "What does 'hmmm' mean?"

" 'Hmmm' is like a sigh that you say out loud. Instead of going, 'sigh' . . . you go, 'hmmm.' "

"Megan Murphy, that's an evasive answer."

"Hah! Talk about evasive."

"What's that supposed to mean?"

"Think about it."

He slung his arm around her shoulders and propelled her toward the house. He didn't have to think about it. He knew exactly what Megan was referring to. They were lovers and friends, and they flirted with the idea of being engaged. They even went so far as to pretend they were engaged, but they weren't engaged. He'd never asked, and she'd never answered, and there'd never been an exchange of commitments.

For the first time in his life he found his supply of easy confidence rapidly dwindling. Med school had been hard, and internship even harder. Now he was on his own with a fledgling practice and a fistful of debts. He wasn't sure he could afford the responsibility of a wife and child. Even if he could afford a family, he wondered if he'd have the time to be a good father and husband. In a year or two he might be able to take on a partner. Until then his case load would become more and more demanding. And as if that weren't enough, he was genuinely worried about the "hmmm."

They looked sideways at each other, silently

questioning, debating, the wisdom of their involvement.

Pat was the first to turn away. "How about some coffee?"

At two o'clock Megan and her parents arrived at Pat's cottage. Megan had dressed casually, in soft brown leather boots, a long, full camel skirt, and a crisp white shirt, accented by an outrageously expensive russet-and-black print scarf. She brushed imaginary lint from her black coat while they waited for Pat to answer the door. She was nervous. She wanted everything to be perfect and she didn't have a clue as to how to preside over a turkey dinner.

She almost swooned when she entered the cottage. The aroma of roast turkey, savory dressing, and baking sweet potatoes mingled with the rich, smoky smell of the fire crackling in the fireplace. The autumn sky was gunmetal gray, but inside, the little house glowed with the patina of polished pewter chandeliers and copper kettles.

A folding table had been taken from its storage spot in the shed. Now it stretched almost the entire length of the living area, covered with a freshly ironed white linen tablecloth, periodically interspersed with candlesticks and clusters of yellow mums.

Pat took her coat and handed her a cup of eggnog. "It's traditional in my family that Thanksgiving heralds in the eggnog season. It's my mom's special recipe."

Fresh-ground nutmeg floated on top of the creamy drink, and its spicy smell reminded Megan that Christmas was just a month away. She gazed around the restored cottage fairly bursting with happy people and had a vision of what this house would be like at Christmas, decorated with fresh holly and red velvet bows.

It would be the perfect place to be married, she thought. She didn't want to walk down a long church aisle in an extravagant gown. She wanted to stand in front of the huge fireplace, wearing a romantic lacy dress, surrounded by family, and exchange vows. She wanted to be married in a house that smelled like turkey and dressing, and she wanted her private marriage ceremony to be followed by a terrific party.

Pat's mother hugged her hello and pulled her to the stove. "You have to see the bird.

It's magnificent. It's a monster!" She opened the oven door to display the deeply browned turkey, enveloping Megan and twelve other curious onlookers in a rush of heat.

She gasped at the enormous creature. It was a beast, sitting in simmering splendor, disgorging stuffing from between its colossal drumsticks.

"I think I overstuffed it," Mrs. Hunter said. "Pat stitched it up with his best surgical skills, but the darn thing split open about half an hour ago." She lovingly basted it and shut it back up in the oven.

The big brown rabbit hopped across Megan's feet, with Pat's nephew in hot pursuit. Timmy gurgled happily from his new walker as he scooted backward over the kitchen floor. A football game could be heard blasting from the television in the bedroom overhead, and Megan helped Laurie fix a platter of crackers and cheese and carried it to the circle of women by the fireplace.

She was able to watch Pat from a distance. His face was flushed from the heat of the kitchen and the excitement of the day. He stooped to give Timmy a kiss while picking up a dropped toy. He surreptitiously took a small swipe of whipped cream from a pumpkin pie and carried a six-pack of cold beer up the stairs.

He was wonderful, she thought. Second only to the turkey, and when the turkey was picked clean, Pat would be the most edible dish in town.

The oven buzzer rang, and they all jumped to their feet. Laurie poked the potatoes bubbling in a caldron on the stove. "Done!" She picked up the electric mixer and stood there poised, ready for mashing.

Mrs. Hunter stabbed the turkey at the juncture of the thigh. "Done!"

Megan's mother punctured a baked sweet potato. "Done!"

All action stopped while the women stared at the turkey.

"It's big," Megan's mother said.

Mrs. Hunter worried her bottom lip. "The butcher said twenty-seven pounds, but I don't believe him. Looks more like fifty."

Mrs. Murphy had two big meat forks in her hands, but she didn't make a move to lift the turkey. "How the devil are we going to get it onto the platter?"

"Well," Pat's sister Laurie said, "Pat bought it. I think he should be given the honor."

Everyone agreed. It was Pat's job.

"Hey, Pat," Megan yelled up the stairs. "You're needed in the kitchen for bird transfer."

All the men trooped downstairs.

"No sweat," Pat said. "Obviously, this is one of those things that requires a man's cool head and brute strength." He surveyed the bird and stabbed its midsection with the two forks. "Hold the platter," he instructed his brother. "Hold the rack," he instructed his father.

He raised the bird a fraction of an inch and moved it forward. The turkey rotated on the forks, its tender meat disintegrating around the tines, and the beast dropped with a loud thunk onto the open oven door. It jumped off the door and skittered across the kitchen floor, coming to rest toe to toe with Timmy.

"Brrrph," Timmy said.

Megan's mother never batted an eye. She set the platter on the floor, grabbed the turkey stem to stern, and hefted it onto the dish with a loud grunt. "Hardly touched the floor. And the thirty-second rule's in effect. Good thing this floor's clean," she said.

Pat's nephew's eyes got as big as golf balls. "Oh, neat. It left a grease trail. Looks like slug slime!"

Pat's niece wrinkled her nose. "Yuk. It fell on the floor! Now it has rabbit cooties. I'm not eating it. Not one single bite. You can't make me eat rabbit cooties."

Pat lifted the bird onto the table and grinned. "And to think I was worried something would go wrong today. Silly me."

When everyone was seated, Pat carved from the top of the turkey, swearing to his niece by the Hippocratic oath that it was impossible for the top of the turkey to have rabbit cooties.

They worked through the mountains of potatoes, sampled all the vegetables, polished off the spoon bread, and ate and ate and ate, but they didn't make a dent in the turkey. Even after second and third helpings, it was obvious someone would be eating leftover turkey for a very long time.

Megan looked down the table at the butchered carcass and contemplated a marriage ceremony that went: through good times and bad times, in sickness and in health, turkey soup, turkey salad, turkey croquettes . . . till death do us part.

Maybe she should reconsider her relationship with Pat. She could put up with his bizarre sense of humor, and she could live with his rabbit. She wasn't sure if she could handle the turkey leftovers.

The turkey was replaced by four different kinds of pie, Indian pudding, gingerbread cookies, pecan bars, and the King's Arms' fig ice cream. After sampling nearly everything, Megan pushed her chair back and groaned. "I can't eat another bite."

Pat's nephew burped. " 'Scuse me," he said. "This was great."

"We should do this again at Christmas," Megan's mother said. "We'll get a nice big Virginia baked ham."

"Yeah!" Pat's nephew shouted. "And Uncle Pat can make it slime across the floor. Boy, that was so cool."

"What about the wedding?" Pat's niece asked. "When is the wedding? Will I be a flower girl?"

Pat pretended to be serious. "The bride decides things like that."

Megan wanted to kick him a good one under the table, but he was half a mile away, at the opposite end.

Everyone turned to her, waiting for an answer. She narrowed her eyes at Pat, who was obviously exerting every ounce of self-control he possessed to keep from bursting out laughing.

"Well," she said evenly, "I thought we'd have the wedding Christmas Eve." She smiled at the little girl. "I'd be honored to have you as flower girl."

Pat grimaced. Terrific, he thought. Now she'd set a date. This was like playing Monopoly, moving your pieces around the board. What would happen when they got to GO? Would they collect two hundred dollars? Or would they actually get married? He saw a look of triumph flit across Megan's face, and thought she looked as if she'd just bought Boardwalk.

He was losing the battle of one-upmanship. He was also getting sucked further into his meddling mother's fantasy. The time was fast approaching when he was going to have to decide if it was his fantasy too.

After the dishes were loaded into the dishwasher, the pots were scrubbed, the food was refrigerated, and the banquet table was folded up and stored in the shed, Pat's

133

brother and his family said their good-byes and returned to their hotel room. Timmy was bedded down, Pat's three sisters went off in search of night life, and the four parents sat enjoying the hypnotic sizzle of the fire.

Pat held out Megan's black coat for her. "Megan Murphy, would you like to go for a walk?"

"Is this a hint? Do I need exercise? Has the pumpkin pie started appearing on my thighs already?"

"You bet it's a hint. But not about pumpkin pie. It's about hugs and kisses and privacy for lovers." He zipped his leather jacket and wrapped a scarf around his neck. "It's about a romantic moonlight stroll through Colonial Williamsburg."

They walked east on Nicholson Street. A horse whinnied in the distance. A low haze of smoke from fireplaces hung at roof level. It had been a gray day, and was a black night, with a thick bank of clouds obscuring the moon and the stars. They walked in silence, holding hands, enjoying each other's company. They strolled past the public jail, and the Coke-Garrett House at the corner of Nicholson and

Waller. Candles flickered in the windows of Campbell's Tavern.

"That would be a nice place for a wedding," Pat said, pointing to the tavern. As soon as he said it, he stopped dead in his tracks. "Oh, damn, now they've got me doing it!"

Megan huddled deeper into her coat. "Do you want to talk about it?"

"Do you?"

"No!" she practically shouted. If they talked about it, they'd have to *do* something about it. The idea of getting married simultaneously pleased her and terrified her. Deep down, she wanted Pat to propose to her, but she didn't want to give him an answer.

They followed the dirt path that led around the Capitol building. Oxen lowed not far off, and Megan wondered where the oxen and horses were stabled for the night. She liked animals. When she settled down she was going to have a whole passel of them. One of everything. A dog, a cat, a horse, a rhinoceros.

There was a horse on her rented farm, but she didn't get to see much of it. It kept to itself in the far reaches of the pasture or hid in the barn. Its owner came regularly to feed and groom it, but she never rode it. Megan didn't know much about horses, but this one looked sluggish and obese, with a big barrel belly and sleepy eyes.

"Do you know anything about horses?" she asked Pat.

"I know one when I see one."

She linked her arm through his. "There's this horse living in my barn."

"I've seen it from a distance."

"There's something odd about it. I don't think it feels well, and it looks much too fat. Someday I'm going to have a horse, and I'm going to keep him nice and sleek."

Pat couldn't help wondering if she intended to have children riding on this sleek horse. And did she expect those children to be his? She didn't want to discuss their trumped-up wedding, but she wasn't denying it as a possibility, either. He suspected they were both struggling through the twilight zone of self-doubt, coming at the problem from opposite ends. Something in her past had turned her against marriage, and many things in his future gave him cause for concern.

He watched the bobbing lights of a

Lanthorn tour making its way down Duke of Gloucester Street and slipped his arm around Megan's shoulders. He was reluctant to start a conversation that might provoke questions he'd rather not answer just then, but his curiosity was getting the better of him.

"Megan Murphy, why are you against marriage?"

"I thought we weren't going to talk about this."

"We're not going to talk about *our* marriage. We're just going to talk about marriage in general."

"I'm not against marriage," she said. "I think marriage is great. It's just not great for me."

"Is this a recent decision? Do I detect a broken heart hanging in your closet?"

"How do you know about my closet? Have you been snooping?"

Pat stopped in front of the apothecary shop and faced her. "It's an expression, Megan. Just an expression. What the devil have you got in your closet, anyway?"

"Never mind about my closet." She tipped her face up into the cold air and walked away from him. "And I don't have a broken heart," she said over her shoulder. "I've been engaged three times, and I didn't love any of them enough to get a broken heart. Maybe it got a little cracked and shrunken, but it never broke."

Pat had to jog to catch her. "Three times?"

"Probably we shouldn't count the first time. I was five years old, and I got engaged to Jimmy Fee. Two weeks later I caught him carrying Mary Lee Barnard's lunch box for her. It's just that it set a precedent."

Was she serious? he wondered. A precedent at five years old? He was in love with a crazy person.

"My senior year in college," she went on, "I got engaged to Steve. I didn't really want to get married, and I especially didn't want to get married to Steve, but my parents kept pushing.

"There was this philosophy in my house that a girl went to college to catch a husband. If you didn't get him by the time you graduated, you were destined for spinsterhood and you'd wasted your parents' hard-earned money on a mere education.

"I can't even remember how it happened,

but suddenly I was engaged. Fortunately, Steve realized his error and skipped town. Took the ring off my finger one day when I fell asleep in the library and left me a note saying he was joining the foreign legion.

"Then there was Dave. My parents thought Dave was the best thing since macaroni. Dave wasn't really such a bad guy. It's just that he was in love with my parents, not me. He liked my mom's cooking and my dad's choice of television shows.

"We got all the way to the altar. I stood there in my white satin gown with twelve hundred seed pearls embroidered on the bodice, in front of an audience of two hundred friends and relatives, and I turned to Dave and wondered what on earth I was doing there. Dave looked at me, then walked down the aisle and out of the church. Two days later he came over to the house to apologize and watch the ball game with my dad."

"Are you making this up?" Pat asked.

Her eyes filled with tears. "It was awful."

He gathered her into his arms and held her close, not knowing what to say. The thought of Megan's being left at the altar made his stomach contract into painful knots. He stroked her silky red hair and rested his chin against her head. He wanted to ask her to marry him. He wanted to ask her to come live in his little cottage, where he could keep her safe and secure and loved, but he was afraid of committing the very crime he wanted to prevent. He was afraid he'd hurt her. He wasn't going to make a very good husband for the next two years.

What were the alternatives? Break off with her? He'd sooner chop off an arm or a leg. A prolonged engagement? If things didn't work out it would be the third time she'd had to give back a ring. He couldn't do that to her. Live together? Nope. He was a pediatrician in a small town. He had to set an example. They could be friends. They could have a long, old-fashioned courtship. He sighed. They were way past courtship. "Oh, hell."

She snuggled into him. "Don't worry about Dave. I'm fine now. It all worked out for the best."

"Damn right. If you'd married Dave, I'd have to eat all those turkey leftovers by myself."

Megan pulled away. She slid her hand into his and started down Duke of Gloucester

Street. He was a slippery one, she thought. He was a master at extricating himself from tender moments. They'd talked about her past, but they hadn't talked about his. She was beginning to wonder how many women Patrick Hunter had left at the altar.

"You ever been engaged?"

"Nope."

A horrible possibility flashed through her mind. "You ever been married?"

"No."

"Why not?"

He shrugged. "No time. No money." He squeezed her hand. "No Megan."

"Hmmm."

"There's that 'hmmm' again. Am I in trouble?"

She smiled. "No. That was a good 'hmmm.' You gave all the right answers."

"You suppose your parents would mind if you spent the night with me?"

"Get serious."

He motioned to the gate of the Botetourt Street garden. "Want to do some necking in the garden?"

She peeked over the red brick fence at a

141

Doberman. "I don't think that's such a good idea."

"This is tough."

"What's the plan for tomorrow? Will you be bringing Timmy over in the morning?"

"Yes. Everyone's driving to Washington to be tourists." His eyes lit up. "No one will be here all day! We could have a sexfest."

"As much as I'd like to, I can't just leave my parents to have a sexfest. Besides, you work tomorrow."

"You could bring Timmy back to my house at six. We could have a short sexfest."

Megan wasn't sure she wanted a short sexfest. The more Pat dragged his feet and evaded proposing, the more she wanted to get married.

Chapter 8

Megan let herself into Pat's dark house and unbundled Timmy. She set him in the walker, made a fire in the fireplace, and lit every light she could find.

"It's a drizzly, dreary night," she told Timmy. "We've got to zap a little cozy into it."

She made a pot of coffee and set it on the kitchen table. She didn't want to drink it. She just wanted to smell it.

"Better. Much better. I think we've succeeded in the cozy department."

She snitched a piece of turkey from the fridge and started Timmy's supper heating.

Ten minutes later Pat came home. "This house is so nice. It's miserable outside, and my house is all warm and—"

"Cozy?"

"Yeah. Cozy." He pulled Megan to him and kissed her hungrily. This wasn't such a bad arrangement, he thought. It was like rent-a-family. He was getting all the benefits of a warm house and warm bed without paying the price of everlasting responsibility. He was chagrined to find it not entirely satisfactory. Deep down, he wanted everlasting responsibility.

"Are you here for a short sexfest?"

She pushed him away playfully. "Crickey, Pat, not in front of the baby. All you think about anymore is S-E-X."

"It's not all I think about, but I have to admit, it's been at the front of my mind a lot lately."

Megan had similar mind problems. Especially after being kissed like that. Good thing Timmy was clattering across the floor in his walker, she thought, because she was putty in Patrick Hunter's hands. Timmy was a loud reminder that there were important things to be discussed.

"Maybe we should be talking instead of sexfesting."

Pat nodded in agreement. So much for rent-a-family, he thought. Besides, she was right. They'd procrastinated long enough. Maybe if they talked about their relationship, they'd find a solution. At least they'd know where they stood.

They both groaned at the knock on the door. "What are the chances that's your mother?" Pat asked. "She's probably come to tell us she's hired a hall and a caterer."

Megan had to smile. At least Pat knew he was being railroaded and could joke about it. That put him one up on Steve and Dave. She opened the door and gasped. It was Tilly Coogan.

The young girl frantically looked around, saw Timmy, and ran to him. She lifted him out of the walker and hugged him and kissed him. She turned to Megan with tears streaming down her face. "I've missed him," she said simply.

"Mum, mum, mum," Timmy shouted.

Megan reached out to Pat for support. She couldn't believe this was happening. She'd convinced herself Tilly wouldn't be back. She'd been thinking about marriage . . . adoption. She'd learned nursery rhymes and bought books on child rearing. She knew how to play eensy weensy spider. How dare Tilly Coogan come back to claim her baby after abandoning him?

Megan felt her temper flare and just as quickly dissipate. Tilly hadn't abandoned Timmy. She'd temporarily entrusted him to the care of her pediatrician.

Megan was left with a painful emptiness in her chest where the anger had been. She noticed a young man standing in the doorway. "Are you with Tilly?"

"Yes, ma'am," he said softly.

Tilly wiped the tears away with the heel of her hand. "I'm sorry. It was rude of me not to make introductions. It's just that I've been so lonesome for Timmy. I knew he was in good hands, but I've still been awful lonesome."

She kissed Timmy on the top of his downy head and pointed to the young man, now awkwardly standing beside her.

"This is Timmy's daddy, Leonard Bell. Lenny, this is Dr. and Mrs. Hunter."

"Pleased to meet you," Leonard said shyly. "It was very nice of you to take care of Timmy. I'm sorry to have caused everyone so much trouble." He stared, wide-eyed, at the little boy. "Til, he's beautiful."

Tilly beamed. "I've done a good job of bringing him up. He knows all kinds of things, and he's healthy, too. You're going to be proud of him, Lenny."

Megan thought if Lenny got any prouder he'd explode. "So," she said, making a supreme attempt to still the tremor in her voice, "what's going on here?"

Tilly took a deep breath and closed her eyes, as if what she was about to say was so wonderful, she couldn't believe she was saying it. "We're getting married."

Lenny looked affectionately at Tilly. "I guess we owe you folks some explanations. Tilly and I have been sweethearts ever since seventh grade. I asked her to marry me when we graduated from high school, but she said no. She said we were too young to get married, so I got myself into a snit and went and joined the Navy."

"Then I found out I was pregnant," Tilly said. She fumbled with the collar of Timmy's terry-cloth pajamas. "I thought I was being so smart, saying we shouldn't get married until we grew up more, but I wasn't smart enough not to get pregnant. When I found out about the baby, Lenny was halfway around the world. I couldn't go to him anyway. We'd had a terrible fight."

She moved into the reassuring arm Lenny held out to her. "I felt I was an embarrassment to everyone. I couldn't bring myself to have an abortion, and I didn't want my mom and my grandma to know I was pregnant . . . so I left. I said I was going north to get a job."

She raised her chin a fraction of an inch. "I think I did pretty good, too. I waited tables until I was ready to deliver, and then afterward I tried to make money typing term papers, so I could be home with Timmy.

"Two weeks ago I got a phone call from Lenny. My mom gave him my cell phone number. He said his ship had finally come home and he still wanted to marry me. Can you imagine? After all that time, and he didn't even know about Timmy. No one knew. Lenny still wanted to marry *me*."

He hugged her to him. "I should have written when I was away, but I'm not much good at that sort of thing."

Tilly looked at Pat with apologetic eyes. "I had to go home to explain to my mom and my grandma and to see Lenny. I couldn't take the baby until I'd made sure everything was okay. I had to be sure Lenny really loved me. I guess I wasn't thinking so good, but I just had to get home and straighten my life out."

Pat could feel Megan's cold hand holding tightly to his, and his heart went out to her. She'd let herself love Timmy, and now she was losing her baby. He wanted to reassure her that Timmy would be well cared for. He wanted to give her a little more time to adjust. "What did your mom and grandma say about Timmy?"

Tilly's face broke into a wide grin. "They were so excited, they didn't know whether to laugh or to cry. Boy, I was really dumb to go off on my own like that. I didn't understand much about love. You don't stop loving someone just because they make a mistake."

"We're packing up Tilly's apartment now," Lenny said. "Then we're going back to Louisiana, and we're going to get married right away. Tilly's going to live with her mom, until I get out of the Navy."

Megan compressed her lips. She didn't want to meddle, but she couldn't help worrying about Timmy. "What about a job? Will you be able to take care of a family?"

"Yes, ma'am. I've learned all about computers in the Navy. I'll be able to get a good job when I get out."

Megan looked around at the toys and books and baby furniture. "Timmy has so many things here," she said absently, resigning herself to the finality of it, feeling utterly lost.

Pat gave Tilly her son's snowsuit. "You can get Timmy dressed, and I'll pack his clothes."

In a matter of minutes Pat had assembled several bags of baby paraphernalia. He handed Timmy his favorite blanket and kissed him. "We're going to miss you, kid." He turned to Megan. "Meg, would you like to kiss Timmy good-bye?"

She shook her head. It would be too painful to kiss him good-bye. She stood with her arms tightly clasped across her chest. She was afraid to move or speak for fear of bursting into tears. Tilly and Lenny seemed like nice people. This was a happy time for them. She didn't want to ruin it, and she didn't want to embarrass herself. It had been foolish of her to think she could keep Timmy, but she'd followed her heart. Damn, she thought. She was such a dope.

Pat closed the door after Tilly and Lenny and Timmy. "He'll be fine. He belongs with his mother. Now he's even got a father and a grandmother and a great-grandmother."

"I know."

"Doesn't make it hurt any less, does it?"

"No."

Pat looked at the toe of his shoe for a minute, then walked into the kitchen and got a dinner plate.

"What's this?" she asked as he handed it to her.

He grinned. "I thought you might want to smash something."

"Please, I feel foolish enough. . . ."

Actually, she did want to smash something. She realized she was practically smothering in anger. It wasn't fair. Every time she made a real commitment to someone, he left her. She hefted the plate and threw it at the fireplace. It smashed, and shards of china scattered on the hearth and braided rug.

"Feel better? Pat asked.

"No."

He shoved his hands in his pockets. This could get expensive, he thought. Megan looked mad enough to go through a service for forty. "Want another plate?"

What she wanted was another baby, Megan realized. She liked being a mother. She was just getting good at it. She didn't want to go back to being a single person, rattling around in the big old farmhouse by herself.

She looked at Pat and thought a short sexfest might not be such a bad idea. She couldn't have Tilly's baby, but she was pretty sure she could have Pat's. It'd be a terrific baby, too. Cute little nose, big brown eyes, perfect teeth. They should get married, of course, but there was no reason they couldn't get started making a baby right away. Why waste valuable time? If she got pregnant now, she could have a baby by the end of the summer.

The trick was getting Pat to make a baby. He'd been very careful about that sort of thing. She might have to take matters into her own hands, she thought slyly.

Pat uneasily shifted his weight from foot to foot. Megan was looking at him as if he were lunch. No, sir, he thought, life with Megan

Murphy was never dull. He didn't have a clue what was going through her mind, but the look in her eyes raised all the little hairs on the back of his neck. This was a desperate woman. This was a woman on the edge.

"Maybe we should go out to dinner," he suggested. If she was planning a double suicide, they'd be safer in a crowded place. She'd feel better after a good meal, and he'd have a chance to talk to her, reason with her.

Dinner? she thought. Maybe that wasn't such a bad idea. It would give her a chance to really get Pat in the mood. A romantic restaurant. The perfect place for a proposal. Once she got the proposal out of the way, it would be clear sailing to motherhood. She rubbed her hands together in anticipation. This time it was going to work. She wasn't going to get dumped on. She wasn't going to get left at the altar. She was going to get pregnant.

"All right," she said. "Dinner. That's a great idea. Someplace dark and quiet. The darker the better."

Pat swallowed and racked his brain for the noisiest best-lit place in Williamsburg.

"I'm going upstairs to freshen up," Megan

said. "Would you call my parents and tell them I'm going to be later than expected?"

"What are you going to do upstairs?"

"It's of a personal nature."

"You're not too depressed, are you? I mean, you wouldn't jump out a window or anything, would you?"

"Pat, if I jumped out a window, the best I could do would be to break my knees."

"Not if you jumped head first."

"Well, yes, but that would ruin my hair."

That made him feel better. Worrying about your hair was a sign of good mental health. He'd read about it in a mental-health course.

Megan ran up the stairs and checked out the candles, making sure there were fresh tapers in all the holders. Then she turned down the bedcovers and closed the curtains. She didn't want to waste any time once they got back from the restaurant. They'd have a memorable meal, a knock-your-socks-off proposal, then they'd rush back here and jump into bed.

She brushed her hair and applied fresh lipstick and a dusting of blusher. She felt much better, she thought, smoothing her sweater over her hips. She really had her life under control now. Good thing she was such a levelheaded person. Some women would have gone off the deep end over losing a baby, but not her. She was flexible. She could find creative solutions to problems like this.

Pat cleaned up the broken china and doused the fire while he waited for Megan. He looked at the empty crib and felt a surge of sorrow pass through his heart. It had been nice having a baby in the house. Someday he'd have children of his own. A whole pack of them, with dogs and cats and hamsters.

For now, he had to admit, the sadness of losing Timmy was being replaced with a sense of relief. Timmy belonged with Tilly and Lenny. And Patrick Hunter belonged with Megan Murphy, he thought wistfully. That was a tougher problem to solve. At least they no longer had the pressures of an instant family. There really was no reason they had to get married immediately.

He looked toward the stairs and wondered what Megan was doing. Probably in the bathroom, crying her eyes out. She'd seemed a trifle desperate for a few minutes, but he was sure she'd be fine. She wasn't the sort to go to pieces and do something dumb . . . was she?

"Megan," he called, "you okay?"

"I'm fine. Peachy-dandy. I'm almost done here. I'll be right down."

He zipped himself into his jacket and paced in front of the door. They needed to go someplace loud tonight, he decided. Someplace fun. He didn't know any loud, fun places, so he called his answering service and asked for advice.

"Go to the Pit," he was told. "Great chili dogs, and you can drink beer and play darts."

The beer part sounded good, but he didn't know if he wanted to put a sharp object in Megan's hand. But then he told himself he was being stupid. Next he'd be looking for an Ethiopian restaurant; so she'd have to eat with her fingers.

Megan bounced down the stairs. "Here I am. Let's get going. Let's not waste a single minute. Gotta get going and eat, eat, eat."

He looked at her suspiciously. "Why are you so happy? Have you been drinking my after-shave?"

"I like being happy. You wouldn't want me to be a party pooper, would you?"

He put his hand to her forehead. She didn't feel feverish, but her eyes had a feverish glitter to them. "You're sounding a little . . . um, crazy."

She looked insulted. Her lower lip trembled and her eyes flooded with tears. "Boy, that's the thanks I get for trying to be happy. Here I am trying to make the best of things, and you tell me I'm crazy."

Oh, great, Dr. Hunter. Wonderful bedside manner, Pat chided himself. Now he'd made her cry.

"Don't pay any attention to me," he said. "This business with Timmy has me off balance."

She gave him a hug. "Don't worry. I've got it all figured out."

"You do?"

"Trust me."

He smiled lamely. He trusted her . . . but he still wasn't going to let her handle any darts.

He escorted her to his car and watched her crawl across the front seat. He'd gotten his window to stay up, but he still hadn't fixed the passenger door. He slid behind the wheel and turned the key in the ignition. Nothing happened. He tried it again and was treated to a low whimper. He sighed. "It's the battery. I need a new one."

"You need a new car."

"I could get one if I fired my receptionist. I can't make payments on both a car and a receptionist."

They crawled out of Pat's car and into Megan's. Pat tried it three times before it started, with a cough, and backfired. He slowly backed out of the driveway and rumbled down the street. "You need a new muffler," he shouted over the noise.

"I could get one if I stopped eating," she shouted back.

When Pat pulled up to a building lit by gaudy neon lights, her mouth dropped open. "This is dark and quiet?"

"I felt like beer and chili dogs. They make great chili dogs here."

"Okay," she said, "whatever turns you on." She moved closer and slid her hand up his leg. "You are turned on, aren't you?"

"Um, well, I wasn't . . ."

She kissed him just below his ear and gently nipped at his neck. "I hope you'll be turned on later . . . when we go home." She whispered several things she wanted to do to him, and was pleased at the flush rising out of his shirt collar.

It suddenly occurred to her that if they did it in the car, she'd have a head start on the evening. After all, it might not happen the first time. She hadn't calculated the correct time. They might have to do it day and night for an entire month! Besides, she wasn't sure she trusted those sperm. What if they got discouraged and swam the wrong way?

She slid her hand higher and pressed against him. "When was the last time you did it in a car, big boy?" she asked in her most sultry voice.

"Now, Megan . . ."

She tickled his earlobe with her tongue and inched her hand higher on his thigh. She was a woman with a cause, a woman driven by her biological and maternal instincts, and certain rules of the road were suspended in situations like this. She had to be bold.

She took a deep breath and firmly moved her hand over the fast-growing bulge in Pat's trousers. She kissed him hard and lay back on the seat, pulling him down on top of her. "Take me, you animal," she cried, struggling to keep him prone.

"Megan, for Pete's sake, we're in a parking lot!"

"No one will notice."

"Everyone will notice. Especially those three kids looking in the window at us."

She turned her eyes to the window and saw three grinning faces peering in at her.

"Once we get the windows good and fogged, they won't be able to see a thing."

"Megan!"

"Geez, I thought you wanted a sexfest."

"I've never thought of myself as being a stuffy person, but I draw the line at an audience. Why don't we go home and do this?"

"No. Now I feel like a chili dog."

Pat shook his head and sighed. Women could be very strange.

Chapter 9

Megan flounced into the booth with as much dignity as she could muster, the smoochy kissing sounds of three teenage boys still burning in her ears. "You'd think they'd never seen anyone kissing in a car before," she said, whipping her hair over her shoulders. She buried her face in the menu, trying to hide her embarrassment.

This was going to be one of those days. She'd probably get food poisoning next, break her leg leaving the restaurant, and be run over by a truck on the way to the hospital.

"Pat, this entire menu consists of hot dogs."

"It's their specialty."

"Okay," she said, "I think I'll have a hot dog. I'll have number seven."

"Kamikaze Dog? It says here it's topped with everything but Astroturf."

"Sounds great."

He glanced skeptically at her. "If you say so," he murmured, then gave their order to a waitress.

Megan looked around. "The hot dogs must be either good or cheap," she said. "This place is packed."

People stood three deep around the oval bar, chomping on hot dogs, drinking beer, shouting to friends. Two walls were lined with wooden booths, and a small area had been set aside in the rear where a serious dart game was taking place. The room was brightly lit and decorated with college pennants riddled with dart holes, save the William and Mary pennant. Not exactly the atmosphere she'd anticipated for a proposal, but what the heck, she decided. You had to be flexible about these things.

The waitress brought their beers.

Megan folded her hands and leaned forward. "Let's talk."

Pat took a long draft of beer, searching his mind for a safe topic. "I circumcised Roger Bruno today. And Cynthia Kramer fainted when she got her DPT booster."

"I don't want to talk about that."

"Oh."

She lowered her lashes coyly. "Can you think of something else to talk about?"

"The weather hasn't been very good lately."

"Deep-six the weather talk."

Pat wrapped his fingers around his beer glass and concentrated on the specks of foam still clinging to the sides. He suspected Megan wanted to talk about either sex or babies. Not subjects he was eager to approach just then, since he was feeling desperate about both. If she made any more suggestions like the ones in the car, he'd have to cover his lap with his jacket. And babies. He was up to his armpits in babies. He was getting new patients so fast, he couldn't remember their names. He'd never wanted to be that kind of doctor. He wanted to be an old-fashioned family doctor. The kind who recognized his patients on the street and got invited to baptisms and weddings.

Megan looked at Pat with annoyance. He didn't have a clue, she thought. Obviously, she was going to have to take charge of this. It was no big deal, she told herself. People got engaged every day. She herself had been engaged three times. In fact, it would be a refreshing change if she were the one to do the proposing this time. Yes, indeed, this was the century of empowerment, and women were allowed to take the initiative. She wouldn't make a big production out of it. It should be simple, yet romantic. Sincere, but not maudlin.

She took a deep breath. Okay, she was ready. Piece of cake. Simple. She cleared her throat.

"Um . . ."

He gazed at her over the rim of his beer glass.

She took his hand in hers. "Pat, sweetheart—"

" 'Scuse me, folks," the waitress said. "Who was dumb enough to order the Kamikaze Dog?" She plunked plates of hot dogs and potato curls on the table.

Megan raised her hand. "Me."

The waitress dropped an Alka-Seltzer packet on the table. "It comes with the Kamikaze Dog. It's free."

Pat grimaced at Megan's plate. "Is your life insurance paid up?"

Megan ignored the food and retrieved Pat's hand. "Pat, darling, there's something I want to ask you."

"Shoot. Ask for anything. The world is your

oyster. You want a kraut dog? A taco dog? A chocolate dog?"

She blinked. "What? No. I want—"

"Meg . . ." Her silk scarf was dangling in a glob of catsup. "Your scarf."

She ripped the scarf off and stuffed it into her handbag. "I'm trying to ask you something!"

"What? What is it? You want my chili dog, right?"

She narrowed her eyes. That did it, she thought. Phooey on the romantic approach.

"Not even close, Hunter," she shouted. "I want your baby. You want to marry me, or what?"

Pat felt his mouth drop open. He closed it with a snap and hunched over the table. "Megan—"

"Louder," the bartender yelled. "We can't hear."

Megan glanced over at the bar. The crowd of people there was eagerly waiting for an answer. Great, she thought. Another audience.

"Give me a break," she called to the bartender. "A little privacy here, please. This is a tender moment."

She turned her attention back to Pat. "Well,

165

how about it? You want to get married? We could make our own baby. It would be even better than adopting Timmy. And the good part is, no one will take him away from us. We don't have to hire a lawyer or go to court or anything. All we have to do is go to bed!"

"Good Lord, Megan, you're serious. Are you serious?"

"Of course I'm serious," she said in a stage whisper. "You think I go around proposing to people every day?"

You have to handle this delicately, Pat warned himself. She's overwrought about Timmy. She's facing death by hot dog. "Honey, you know I care about you, but—"

"But what?"

"But I . . . this isn't . . ." He ran his hand through his hair. "No."

"No?"

Lord, Hunter, he thought, that was so eloquent. Couldn't you have come up with something better than just "no"? What about all the good reasons why you can't get married right now? What about how you're nuts over her and living alone is agony? What about the fact that she's having hormone hysteria and that's not a sound basis for motherhood? Geez, Hunter, what a time to get tongue-tied.

Megan felt her stomach flip. He didn't want to marry her. It was happening again. And she was so dumb, she hadn't even seen it coming. Just as always.

"Are you feeling okay?" he asked. "You're white as a sheet."

"I was a little faint there for a minute, but I'm fine now. I think it was the hot dog fumes that got to me."

"Megan, I should explain—"

"What's to explain? You don't want to marry me. Hey, you're not the first man who didn't want to marry me. I bet if I tried, I could set a world record for getting unengaged. I'm only sorry I didn't have a ring for you to remove. The other men always took their rings back. I hate to break tradition."

"It's not like that this time. Someday we'll get engaged, and it will be for real, for always."

"Don't patronize me when I'm pouting," she snapped. "The least you can do is let me enjoy being miserable."

A linebacker type waved at them from across the room.

"You know that guy on the other side of the bar?" Pat asked. "He was waving to us, and now I think he's coming over."

Megan swiveled in her seat and squinted through the crowd. Her eyes widened, and she clamped her hand over her mouth. "Holy Kamikaze Hot Dogs. It's Dave."

"Dave who?"

"Dave, the guy who left me at the altar."

"You mean the moron who just walked out of the church? That Dave?"

"That Dave."

Pat watched him walk toward their booth. The guy was about six feet seven, had a shoulder span of approximately four feet, and was missing a neck. Pat wanted to punch him in the nose, but he was afraid he'd have to stand on a chair to do it. "What's he doing here?"

Megan tilted her chin up. "Obviously, he wants to see me. Maybe he's heartbroken and still in love and decided he can't live without me."

Pat made a disgusted face. He couldn't imagine Megan with Dave No-Neck. The man looked like the yuppie version of Bigfoot. A cross between Gentle Ben and Magilla Gorilla stuffed into an oversize cable-knit cotton sweater. If he leaned forward just a bit more he'd step on his hands when he walked. The thought brought a smile to Pat's lips.

Megan clenched her fists under the table. Patrick Hunter was grinning like the Cheshire Cat. He thought this whole thing was pretty funny. Well, she'd show him funny. He didn't want to marry her? Fine! She'd marry someone else. She'd marry *anyone* else. She'd even marry Dave, if she had to.

Dave pushed his way through the crowd and smiled down at Megan.

"Meggy, it's good to see you again." He plucked her from the booth, lifted her a foot off the floor, and kissed her on the forehead. "I hope you're not mad at me."

"Mad at you? Me?" She would have liked to set his toenails on fire someday. "Don't be silly, I'm not mad. Everyone has the right to change his mind. After all, this is a free country, isn't it?"

She slid back into the booth and patted the seat next to her. "Want a hot dog? This is the house specialty." She pushed her Kamikaze

Dog over to him. "I ordered it, but I'm not hungry."

"Hate to see it go to waste," Dave said, and stuffed the thing into his mouth.

Pat closed his eyes and tried not to laugh. Lizzie Borden had nothing on Megan Murphy.

Dave finished the hot dog and slung his arm around Megan. "I guess this little guy is Patrick Hunter. When your mom called his house she got his answering service, and they told us you were here. Lucky for me you got an answering service, Pat."

"Mmmm. Lucky."

Megan made a face at Pat and inched closer to Dave. "Goodness, it certainly is nice to see you again. What brings you to Williamsburg?"

"You, sugar plum. I've missed you, pudding pie."

From the corner of her eye, Megan could see Pat making a gagging gesture. She glared at him and wrapped her arms around Dave's massive biceps. "Looks like you've been staying in shape," she said, squeezing the muscle.

"Hey, you know me. My body is sacred."

Now Megan almost gagged. How could she have forgotten about his sacred body? All those perfect muscles that continually needed to be exercised, analyzed, oiled, and massaged. The bones and blood that demanded red meat, whole grains, vitamins, and minerals, not to mention her mother's famous New York cheesecake. How could she have forgotten about his sacred body? Yuk.

Dave smiled affably at Pat. "Hope I'm not interrupting anything. There isn't anything going on between you two, is there?"

He was big, but he was probably slow, Pat thought. He could probably smash Dave's nose halfway into his head and make it out to the car before Dave caught up with him. No, that wasn't any good. That would leave Megan stranded with the hulk, here.

"Nope. Nothing going on," Megan answered. "I asked him to marry me, but he didn't want to. *Déjà vu.* Guess I'm up for grabs."

"He didn't want to marry you?" Dave asked. "What a jerk." He grinned at Pat. "No offense, Pat."

"Up for grabs?" Pat said to Megan, his voice dangerously quiet.

Megan felt a chill run down her spine, but she pulled herself up straight in her seat.

She refused to be intimidated by this . . . this pediatric Casanova, she thought, angrily flinging her hair over her shoulder.

Pat leaned back against the booth. He'd brought Megan there to have fun and forget about Timmy, but somehow he'd managed to make her feel rejected and angry. And as if things weren't going badly enough, now this humanoid sitting across from him was making sounds like a suitor. He couldn't believe Megan had once been engaged to Mr. Muscle. The man called her pudding pie!

Was pudding pie the same Megan he knew and loved? Was pudding pie the fuming redhead who'd stormed into his kitchen with his rabbit wrapped in her cape? Pat suspected if he ever called Megan pudding pie she'd kick him in the knee.

"Hey, I'd like to do some grabbing," Dave said. "I'm even prepared to pay for my grabs." He reached into his pocket and extracted a small blue velvet case. "Look, sugar, do you know what this is?"

Megan stared at the case dully. It was like reliving a nightmare in broad daylight. Not nearly so scary, but it squeezed her heart and turned it cold.

"Let me guess. Is it a Jeep?"

Dave chuckled. "Nope." He popped the lid open, and the two-carat diamond glittered malevolently at Megan. "It's your old engagement ring. I don't know why I kept it. I guess maybe I always knew someday it'd go back on your finger."

Megan managed a weak smile. She'd have her finger amputated before she put that ring back on it.

"Gee, Dave, I hardly know what to say. Is this a proposal? Hear that, Pat? Dave just proposed to me."

Pat signaled to the waitress. "We're celebrating a proposal here. This gentleman would like two more 'K' Dogs. My treat."

"You're okay," Dave said, grinning. "He's a nice guy," he told Megan.

"Hmmm," Megan said.

Dave leaned across the table. "Just between you and me, why didn't you want to marry her?"

Pat looked at him very calmly. "She's

pregnant. She just asked me to marry her so the baby would have a father."

"No kidding. Is it your cake in her oven?"

Pat shook his head. "No way."

Megan was speechless. She felt her jaw go slack, her eyes pop out, and her adrenal glands take a brief pause before declaring code red. "That is . . . I . . . you . . ." she sputtered, jumping to her feet.

"It's common for pregnant women to stutter and get overly emotional," Pat said to Dave. "I know about these things. I'm a doctor."

"A doctor? No joke? Boy, that's great."

"I'm *not* pregnant," Megan shouted.

"Denial," Pat whispered to Dave. "That's stage one when you have an unwed mother."

Dave shook his head. "This is sad. I never expected it."

Pat punched him lightly on the biceps. "Don't worry about it. You're going to make a terrific father."

"I don't know. I wasn't counting on marrying somebody who's already pregnant with someone else's kid."

"Dave," Pat said, his voice soft and pleading, "someone's got to marry her. Be a sport."

"Hell, why don't you marry her, if you're such a bleeding heart?"

"It would be easier for you. You've already got a ring." Pat stood up and turned his pockets inside out. "You see? No ring."

"I'll sell you this one."

He shook his head. "I couldn't afford a ring that size."

"I'll give you a good price. It has a flaw in it."

"What?" Megan shrieked. "You gave me a ring with a flaw in it? You told me it was perfect. 'Perfect like me,' you said."

"That's how she got pregnant," Pat confided in Dave. "Believes everything she's told. Right off the pumpkin truck."

"Sad," Dave said.

"So who's gonna marry her?" the waitress asked.

"Yeah," the bartender called. "Which one of you guys is gonna marry her?"

Megan folded her arms across her chest and tapped her foot. Count to ten, she told herself. This wasn't really happening.

"Tell you what," Dave said. "We'll settle this man to man. I'll arm-wrestle you for her. Loser has to marry her."

"Oh, no. That's not a fair contest. You've eaten more spinach than I have. How about a game of chess?"

"I don't play chess. Chess is a wimpy game."

"We got a dart board in the back," the waitress suggested. "How about darts?"

"I guess darts would be okay," Pat said.

Dave laughed. "Man, I'm going to whip your butt at darts."

"Don't worry, pudding pie," Pat whispered to Megan, "I'll try to lose."

Megan reached for his neck, but he was whisked away by the bar crowd.

"Best two out of three games," the bartender pronounced, filling everyone's mug with beer.

Pat took careful aim, let sail, and hit a bull's eye. His second dart hit number seven on the inside ring. The third dart sliced into the bull's eye again.

A roar went up from the crowd.

"You're a dart hustler!" Dave yelled, red-faced. "You're a lousy dart shark."

Megan wrung her hands. "I thought you said you'd lose," she hissed to Pat.

Dave stepped up to the mark, wiped his

hands on his shirt, and completely missed the dart board on his first throw. "This doesn't count, right? This is just a practice game?" He slugged down a beer and hit the bull's eye with his second and third dart.

The second round was a tie.

Pat retrieved the darts, took a sip of beer, and stood poised to throw.

"I'm not going to look," Dave said, flushed from beer and the third Kamikaze Dog. He stood next to the dart board, his face pressed to the wall and his hands covering his ears. "Tell me when it's over."

Pat aimed his dart and winked at Megan. The dart left his hand with a snap of his wrist. It arced gracefully in the air, then dropped short just as Dave uncovered his eyes and lurched toward the board.

There was a moment of stunned silence in the bar before Dave started screaming. "Yeow!" he shrieked. "I've been stabbed!" He looked over his shoulder and gaped at the silver dart sunk a good inch and a half into his right buttock. "Somebody help me," he pleaded. "Call a doctor."

"I'm a doctor," Pat said. "Do you have

medical coverage? Do you know your group number?"

"Get this madman away from me! He tried to kill me. You tried to kill me!"

Megan rolled her eyes. "Good grief, Dave. He didn't try to kill you. It's just a dart, for crying out loud."

"It was a mistake," Pat said, smiling pleasantly. "It slipped out of my hand just as you moved over."

"Someone pull the damn thing out," Dave cried. "I'm in pain! Lord, I feel sick. I'm gonna barf."

"Three Kamikaze Dogs," the waitress explained to the bartender.

"Don't be such a baby," Megan said, and yanked the dart from his backside.

The bartender produced a first-aid kit. "You want a Band-Aid, or something?"

Pat selected a bottle. "A little peroxide and a Band-Aid, and you'll be good as new, Dave."

"Forget it," Dave snarled. "I'm not dropping my pants for you . . . you pervert."

"We should take him to the emergency room," Pat said. "He should have a tetanus shot."

Megan bowed her head and bit her lip to keep from laughing. She was furious at both of them, but she had to admit, it was funny. Pat was very solicitously playing the role of doctor, and Dave had deserved a dart in the butt.

"I'm not going to any hospital," Dave said. He took a step forward and stopped. "I can't walk." He hobbled a little farther. "What am I going to do? I'll never be able to drive."

"Maybe we can lie him across the back seat of my car," Megan said.

Pat looked doubtful. "I think he's too big, but we could probably strap him to the roof."

Dave looked as if he might cry. "I feel sick. I gotta get some air."

"Sad," Pat said, as Dave limped toward the door. "His body used to be sacred."

Megan marched after Dave. "You're the one who's sad, Patrick Hunter," she said as Pat hurried after her. "I can't believe you did that! Stabbing an innocent man with a dart. Letting your childish temper get the best of you."

"It was an accident. He staggered right in front of the dart board."

"You winked at me. You knew perfectly well what you were doing."

Pat looked offended. "I was flirting."

"Flirting? With a pregnant woman? You humiliated me. He asked me to marry him, and you told him I was pregnant. You ruined everything."

Pat made an outraged grunt. "What was I supposed to do, sit there and watch you get engaged to Bluto?"

"You had no business interfering."

"Egads, will you two hold it down?" Dave said, struggling to the curb. "Megan, where's your car?"

"It's this maroon thing right in front of you."

"What happened to your Carrera?"

Pat frowned. Megan Murphy owned an expensive sports car? No, he thought, pudding pie owned an expensive sports car.

"I sold it to buy a kiln," she said.

She opened the back door and felt a pang of genuine sympathy for Dave as he painfully crawled across the seat. He really couldn't help being a moron, she thought, and he was hurting. His perfect body had been violated. Like Barbie dolls and blue nail polish, Dave was a discarded part of her past, and she didn't want to hate him. She'd rather file him away with Mr. Potato Head, wondering from time to time what the attraction had been.

Half the restaurant had followed them outside, and everyone gave directions. "Bend your knees, scoot up a bit, watch your head when we close the door." Then they all waved good-bye as the car belched an acrid blast of exhaust and pulled out of the parking lot.

Megan looked at Dave in her rearview mirror. "Where to?"

"I don't know. I thought I'd be staying with you."

"Oh, great." She stopped for a light and massaged her temples.

"Headache?" Pat asked. "Need a doctor?"

"I don't need a maniacal pediatrician," she said stiffly, turning onto Nicholson Street. She parked in front of Pat's cottage. "Out."

"Don't you think it would be best if I went home with you and helped get Dave settled on the couch?"

"My dear mother will help with that." She pointed to the door: "Out!"

Pat stood at the curb and watched her roar away. She was mad, he thought. Hell hath no fury like a woman scorned. He hadn't meant to scorn her. He'd only wanted to slow things down a bit. Then dopey Dave had showed up. Now dopey Dave was going home with her.

Pat kicked his front step and tore the sutures out of his shoe, causing his little toe to pop out. Swell. After paying for three Kamikaze Dogs he was left with only spare change in his pocket, and now he needed shoes. How could he afford a wife, when he couldn't even buy shoes?

Megan motored out of the historic area and turned toward home. Thank goodness it was dark and Dave was flat on his stomach, Megan thought, blinking back tears. She didn't want to share her grief with anyone. There had been too many public displays of emotion in her life. She needed to cry in private this time. This love affair had been special. This time she had fallen in love with a man *she* had chosen. Steve and Dave had humiliated her, but Pat had broken her heart.

"Meggy," Dave called from the back seat, "are you really pregnant?"

"No."

"Why did Pat say you were pregnant?"

She sniffled. "He has a weird sense of humor."

"I think he's in love with you."

"Sometimes love isn't enough."

Dave sighed. "I know. I loved you, but I couldn't marry you."

"You never loved me, Dave. You loved my mother and father. You loved my car. You loved being in love but you never loved me. You didn't even know who I was. You loved some fantasy person called pudding pie. That's why you couldn't marry me."

Dave was silent for a moment. "You're pretty smart, Meggy," he finally said.

Yeah, she thought. But if she was so smart, why was she so stupid? In a half hour she'd have Dave tucked away on her couch, and she'd be alone in her room, crying her eyes out. She'd lost her whole instant family. No more pretend baby. No more pretend husband.

She knew from past experiences that her best defense against pain was anger. If she stayed angry, she could use that energy to survive. After a time, the pain would diffuse and the anger could be discarded. That was how it had been with Steve and Dave. That was how it would be with Pat.

Chapter 10

Pat opened his eyes and sighed. No Megan Murphy in his bed. No Timmy downstairs waiting for breakfast. No reason to wake up. He closed his eyes, but he couldn't go back to sleep. *Ridiculous*, he thought. *It's a beautiful day, Hunter. Look at that blue sky. Look at that sunshine.*

He sat up and swung his legs over the side of the bed, wriggling his bare toes in the carpet. *Things could be a lot worse, you know,* an inner voice said. *You could be poor Dave and have a dart hole in your backside.* Hah! Pat answered his inner voice. *Poor Dave is stretched out on Megan's couch. You don't see poor Dave waking up in an empty, lonely house, do you?*

Several hours later, Pat was still sulking as he led his family down Duke of Gloucester Street. They'd visited the cooper, the boot maker, the milliner, and the silversmith, but there was no sign of Megan. Pat had a miserable feeling that she was at home with Dave. So what if she was at home with Dave? Her parents were there, right? What could happen with her parents there? Besides, Dave wasn't exactly in shape to be romantic. He might even have an infection by now. Probably he could use an antibiotic. Better go check it out, Pat decided. After all, it was his fault, and he wouldn't want complications to set in.

"I have a medical emergency to attend to," he told his family. "I'll only be gone a short time. You can have lunch while I'm off doctoring."

He pointed them in the direction of Christiana Campbell's Tavern and ran down the path leading to Nicholson Street. He slid behind the wheel of his car, held his breath, and turned the key. Yes! The battery had been baking in the sun and was feeling cooperative.

He slowly chugged out of the historic district and stopped for a red light while he rehearsed his opening line. Hello, Megan, just thought I'd stop by to see how Dave's duff is doing. Then what? Blank space. He didn't know then what.

He gripped the wheel more tightly. He'd

explain to her about marriage and about being a new doctor. They couldn't live on his salary. *What about her salary?* the inner voice suggested. *If you combined your incomes and only had one house payment?*

He shook his head. It wouldn't work. He was too busy. She'd feel ignored and resentful of his patients. *Baloney,* the voice said, she's just as busy as you. *She'd match you pot for patient.* But there are other good reasons, Pat argued.

He inhaled sharply as the truth suddenly flashed into his mind. There were no good reasons. He simply wasn't ready to get married. Could that be true?

He pulled to the shoulder of the two-lane country road. He was no better than Dave! He had a rampant case of yellow belly. His hormones were hot, but his feet were cold. Now what? Now that he knew the awful truth about himself, what was he supposed to do? He made a U-turn and headed back to town. He had to think.

Megan heard the tiny bell ringing and stopped in mid-stride. She gritted her teeth, counted to ten, and took a deep breath. "Yes, Dave?"

"Would it be too much trouble to make me a cup of hot chocolate?" he called from his prone position on the couch. "I don't want to bother you. If you're busy you don't have to make it."

"No trouble," Megan said, banging a pot onto the stove. It was one o'clock in the afternoon, and already he'd rung that damn bell seven thousand times. If he rang just once more, she'd cut off his hand, she thought with grim cheer.

"Sure is nice of you to take care of me when I'm crippled like this," he went on. "Too bad your folks had to leave this morning. It was just like old times, having us all together."

Just like old times, she thought with irritation. Her mother had waited on him hand and foot the day before, feeding his sacred body a week's worth of groceries in a matter of hours, and her father had spent the entire day debating the value of the football draft. Now she was left alone with dying Dave, making her own feeble attempt to keep him comfortable and amused.

How long did it take for a dart hole to heal, anyway? The man had spent all day Saturday flat on his stomach. Now it was Sunday, and he was moaning more loudly than ever. This was all Patrick Hunter's fault.

She sloshed some milk into the pot and drummed her fingers on the counter while she waited for it to heat. Patrick Hunter was a no-good rat. First he'd conned her into baby-sitting for Timmy Coogan, and now he'd forced her into baby-sitting for disabled Dave. Patrick Hunter had made her fall in love with him, had lured her into his bed, and then had wimped out. "Men!"

She stormed into the living room and slammed the mug of hot chocolate onto the coffee table. "Anything else?"

"I am a little hungry. . . ."

"Hungry?" she screamed. "There's nothing left. You've eaten it all. All the cereal, all the eggs, all the bread." She heard the crunch of gravel in her driveway and saw Pat's car pass by the window.

She flung the door open at the first knock and scowled at Pat. "What do you want?"

Use the honest approach, he decided. First things first. "I want to know if Dave's here."

"Yes. Dave is here. So what?"

"I don't like it."

"*You* don't like it? Here's a news flash. I don't like it, either, but I can't get him off my stupid couch. The man is in pain. He can't walk. He can't sit. He can't get dressed."

Pat stepped into the house. "He can't get dressed? Are you telling me you've got a naked man on your couch?"

"He's not naked. He's under a blanket, and he's a total pain in the backside, if you'll excuse the expression. I had to play nursey to that bovine boor all day yesterday and half of today, and I've had it up to my earlobes. This is your fault. You did this. You fix it. I want him out! Do something!"

Pat grinned. "Leave it to me. I'll have him fixed up in no time."

"Meggy?" Dave called. "Who is it? It's not that lunatic doctor, is it?"

"Yup," Pat said, walking into the living room. "It's the lunatic doctor. You're a lucky guy. Not many doctors make house calls these days."

"I don't need a doctor."

"Too bad. I brought my little black bag with me, and I'm prepared to relieve your pain. But hey, if you like pain, that's okay with me."

Dave looked interested. "I hate pain."

Pat lifted a corner of the blanket. "Let me just take a peek at this nasty old wound. Hmmm. Not bad. Looks like it's healing okay."

He took a disposable syringe and a small vial from his bag. "This is the magic elixir that's going to get you on your feet. This stuff will get you on the yellow brick road to home."

"What is it, an antibiotic?"

"Novocain."

Fifteen minutes later, Dave stood at the front door with his suitcase in one hand and an inflated rubber doughnut under his arm. "You think it's safe to drive?"

"Absolutely," Pat said.

Megan waved as Dave drove away. "How long will that Novocain last?" she asked Pat.

"About an hour." Pat smiled. "A little pain builds character. Besides, he's got the doughnut, and the wound didn't look serious. He'll be fine."

If a little pain built character, she should be

a wonderful person, Megan thought. Too bad you couldn't take Novocain for a broken heart. She'd been so busy caring for Dave that she hadn't thought much about Pat. Seeing him in her living room, though, had brought all the sadness back.

She'd really wanted to marry him. Underneath all the craziness about making babies and pretending to be Mrs. Hunter was a genuine desire to spend the rest of her life with him. If her love hadn't been so deep and so intense, she could have ambled along, being friends and occasionally lovers. But she couldn't amble with Pat. There would always be the ache of wanting more, and there would always be the bitter knowledge that more wasn't going to happen.

Suddenly, she couldn't bear to look at him. She didn't want to see him. She didn't want to talk to him. She didn't want to hear others talk about him. She'd moved to Williamsburg to escape the memories of Dave, and now she was going to run away from everything associated with Pat. She'd pack up her kiln and go somewhere. Anywhere.

"I have a lot of things to do," she said,

keeping her voice light. "Thank you for taking care of Dave. Good-bye."

"Good-bye?"

"I'm leaving."

"Where are you going? When did you decide this?"

"I don't know where I'm going, and I just decided." She carried the hot-chocolate mug to the kitchen and rinsed it out. "I think I'll move to Alexandria. I sell a lot of my pots there, and it would be closer to the Washington galleries."

She turned on her heel and practically ran up the stairs to her bedroom. Do it, she told herself. Do it before you start blubbering. Do it before you lose your nerve. Do it before you make a complete fool of yourself and beg him to love you. She pulled a suitcase from under the bed and began throwing clothes into it.

Pat stood in the doorway, watching her, thinking she was the most intriguing, beguiling, impossible creature ever made. She looked like a little girl, with her red hair tied up in a fluffy ponytail, but there was nothing little-girlish about the voluptuous body beneath tight faded jeans and a clingy yellow sweater. He was on intimate terms with that body, and the remembrance of evenings past tugged at his heart.

Megan reached into her closet for several blouses, then paused and glared at a long white garment bag. She made a sound of disgust and punched the bag.

"What's in the bag?" Pat asked.

"None of your business," she said, smashing the blouses into the suitcase.

"It's a strange shape for a punching bag."

"If you must know, it's my wedding gown."

His brows rose in surprise. "From Dave?"

"From Dave."

"Why on earth is it hanging in your closet?"

She stopped packing and stared at the gown. "In the beginning, I didn't know what to do with it. It cost a fortune. I couldn't bring myself to throw it away, and I felt foolish pawning it off on the Salvation Army. I was so filled with bitterness that I decided to keep it as a reminder of my own stupidity. I thought as long as I had that gown in my closet I wouldn't make the same mistake again. Pretty sick, huh?"

Pat smiled. "I don't know. You've developed

a decent right hook. You keep that bag around long enough, and we could get you a title bout."

She stuffed a handful of panties into the suitcase, and he carefully rehung a blouse. She emptied her sock drawer into the bag, and he returned the panties to the dresser.

Megan looked at her empty suitcase in amazement. "What are you doing?"

"I'm helping you unpack."

"Don't do me any favors."

He patted her fanny. "You look great in those jeans."

"Hands off!"

He wrapped his arms around her from behind and kissed her neck.

"Pat!"

"I can't help myself. Mmmm, you smell nice."

She wriggled free and snapped her suitcase shut. "I don't need all that stuff anyway. I'll go up for a few days, find a place to live, and then return with a U-haul truck."

"I don't want you to go, Meg. I'm going to miss you."

"I'll miss you, too, but I have to go."

He stalked her around the bed. "Bet I could convince you to stay."

She looked at him warily. There was only one thing that would convince her to stay, and he wasn't referring to that.

"I need a good-bye kiss," he said.

"No good-bye kisses."

He tackled her and flung her, shrieking, onto the bright red patchwork quilt on her bed. He crawled on top of her before she could scramble off, and kissed her quickly.

Megan immediately stopped shrieking and started kissing. They were good-bye kisses from the very bottom of her soul. Good-bye kisses to last a lifetime and store away in her memory. The good-bye kisses of a woman who knew there would be no more lovers in her future.

Pat drew away and touched her cheek with a trembling hand. "You're really going."

"Yes," she whispered, pulling herself to her feet. She took her handbag and carefully walked down the stairs. You can do this, Megan, she told herself. One step at a time. Soon you'll be out the door and into your car, starting life over again.

"Meg, you can't go."

"Why not?"

Why not? Because I love you, he thought, but his mouth wouldn't form the words. "Because . . . because who's going to eat the turkey leftovers?"

Her mouth dropped open; then she snapped it shut. She went straight to her car and climbed in behind the wheel.

Pat groaned. Lord, that was the wrong answer. This was no time to make jokes. The woman of his dreams was leaving. "Megan . . ."

She slammed the door, locked it, and gunned the engine. A shower of stones flew behind her as she peeled out of the yard.

Pat ran to his car and took off after her. He had to talk to her. Make her listen to reason. What was reason? That he was an immature jerk and was afraid to sign on the dotted line?

"Okay," he said, "so I'll sign. I'll sign!" He beeped his horn and waved at her. "Pull over!" he shouted.

Megan gripped the wheel and stepped on the accelerator. The car backfired and the valves clattered in protest, but the machine surged forward.

Pat pressed his own accelerator, but nothing

happened. He was maxed out at thirty-five miles per hour.

"Piece of junk," he muttered, fuming. "Ugly, stupid excuse for a car."

He was relieved to see Megan stopping for traffic ahead. Once she got onto the highway he'd never catch her, but while she was going through the commercial district he had a chance. He stepped on the brake and felt it go clear to the floorboard. He didn't have any brakes!

He blew the horn, pulled on the emergency brake, and swerved to the right at the last instant, but he still slammed into Megan's right rear quarter panel. There was the sound of tearing metal and crunching glass. Pat felt himself thrown forward against his seat belt, then everything was quiet, except for the soothing hiss of steam escaping from his cracked radiator.

He unstrapped himself and ran to Megan. Her car reminded him of a giant maroon accordion. He'd pushed her into a garbage truck, which appeared completely unscathed, but the snout of Megan's car was telescoped into itself. "Megan!"

She looked at him glassy-eyed and blinked slowly. "I said no more kisses."

"Are you okay?" He wrenched the door open and looked for blood, felt for broken bones. "Megan, speak to me!"

She eased out of the crumpled car and stood on wobbly legs. A crowd had gathered around them. A siren wailed in the distance. "What happened?" she asked.

He put a supporting arm around her. "My brakes broke. I couldn't stop."

"Oh, good," she said. "I thought you were mad at me."

An hour later they'd signed all the police reports and grimly watched the cars being towed away. "Don't worry," Pat said. "I have insurance. It'll pay for your car."

Megan sighed. "How are we going to get home?"

"The police officer said he'd give us a ride."

"This has been some day."

Pat nodded. "I'm probably being repaid for sending Dave home on a rubber doughnut. I don't suppose you'd want to come to my house for turkey leftovers."

She shook her head. "I want to go home. I'm

going to take an aspirin and soak in a hot tub, then contemplate my future."

"I'd like to talk to you about your future."

"I don't think I'm ready to talk about it. I feel a little . . . dazed."

When the squad car stopped at Megan's door, Pat got out, too, following his instincts as a doctor more than as a lover. Megan really did seem dazed, and he didn't want to leave her alone. They stood on the porch for a moment, watching the police drive away.

It was mid-afternoon, and the sun was casting long shadows across the yard. A dog yapped in the distance. The tenant horse lounged against the split-rail fence in the far corner of the pasture.

"You're right," Pat said. "That horse is fat."

"I feel like getting fat," Megan said. "I feel like eating fifty pounds of chocolates."

He opened the front door for her. "I'd go get you fifty pounds of chocolates, but I haven't got a car."

Megan felt tears burning behind her eyes. It had all been too much. "I think I need a hug," she whispered.

He tenderly gathered her to him, stroking

her hair, pressing a kiss against her temple. "Why is life so complicated?"

She didn't know. She only knew that she loved him and needed him to hold her. She didn't want to think about tomorrow or next week or next year. She didn't want to think about marriage or babies or bashed-in cars. She wanted to be comforted. She moved closer, fitting herself to him, needing to absorb his warmth, his strength, his affection for her.

"Do you suppose for just one night we can pretend life isn't complicated at all?"

When he answered his eyes were bright, his voice husky. "We can pretend for as long as you like."

This was his fault, he thought. He'd brought this pain to them. He didn't want to lose her, but he couldn't promise to keep her.

He saw a tear catch on her curly red lashes, and kissed it away. Then he lowered his mouth to hers, finding it incredibly soft and warm.

The kiss was deep and intense with the unspoken love that throbbed between them, and Megan gave herself up to it. She could feel her body awakening, anticipating the pleasure, the mindless obsession to please and be pleased.

Pat sensed the difference in her attitude. She no longer needed comforting. She was indulging herself, reveling in the power of her own sensuality, inviting him to join with her. He answered the invitation with a kiss that was hard and urgent.

"So lovely," he whispered. "I'll never tire of you . . . the silky feel of your hair, the taste of your skin, the way you arch your back when my mouth is on you." He was glad he'd smashed her car. What would he do if she left? He couldn't imagine ever desiring another woman. Only Megan.

"Maybe we should go upstairs," he said, taking her hand and starting up the stairs. "What do you think about a long, hot shower?"

She laughed. "I think it sounds lovely, but I'm not sure I have the patience. . . ."

His smile became mysterious as he led her into the bathroom and turned on the water.

"Testing your patience will be a highlight of the evening," he whispered.

She demurely stepped out of her clothes and into the hot shower. With a crook of a finger, she beckoned him to her. "Perhaps we should make this a contest . . . of patience."

They clung to each other, then, as if their physical joining could solve all other problems. They spent the night together, sated and exhausted, under the thick plaid quilt on Megan's bed.

Monday morning Pat kissed Megan awake. "Meg, I have to go to the hospital."

She ran a hand through her long tangle of hair and sat up, tucking the quilt firmly around her bare breasts. She felt better. Depressed but stronger.

"Thank you. It was a very beautiful night."

Pat could only nod. Megan was in control now, he realized. The pretending was over, forever, and he had to leave. "I'll work it out, Meg."

She looked at him coolly. "Me too."

Megan was packing some of her books in a cardboard box when the insurance adjuster arrived with a check for the damages to her car. She looked at the check and blinked. "This check is for one hundred and fifty dollars. The garage said it would cost over a thousand to fix my car."

"Sorry," the adjuster said. "The car's replacement value is only a hundred and fifty dollars."

He left, and she sat on the bottom step, staring at her suitcase, newly packed and ready to go, waiting in the foyer. It was going to have a long wait, she thought. She wasn't going anywhere without a car, and she certainly couldn't buy one with a hundred and fifty dollars.

She continued to sit on the step for a long time, trying to come to terms with her problems, but they skittered through her head like clouds on a windy night. The problems and their solutions were wandering aimlessly in a place where murky emotions reigned.

Finally, her stomach growled, reminding her it was dinner time. She looked in her freezer. Empty. She looked in her refrigerator. Empty. Dave had eaten everything. She couldn't go food shopping, because she didn't have a car. She was going to starve to death. Good. She felt like starving to death. It was pathetic. She found a box of stale crackers and decided to eat them at the kitchen table with a glass of water, because that was even more pathetic than starving to death. She was trying to swallow her third cracker when Pat arrived.

He hadn't bothered to knock. The door had been open, so he'd walked right in and found Megan at the table with the crackers. "Hors d'oeuvres?" he asked.

"Dinner. And when these are done, I'm going to starve to death."

"Life is tough, huh?"

"I think I'm in a slump." She sat up straight and sniffed. "What do I smell? Do I smell turkey?"

He set a brown paper bag on the table. "Turkey, dressing, cranberries, the works. I've been hacking my way through these leftovers for four days now, and I refuse to continue alone. You have to do your share."

"I don't know. I had my heart set on malnutrition."

"You can get malnutrition tomorrow," he said, arranging the food on a dinner plate. He slid the plate into the microwave and sat across from Megan.

"I know I'm going to regret asking, but why were you eating crackers and water?"

"It's all I have. Dave ate everything, and I haven't got a car. I'm trapped here like a rat on a sinking ship."

"I talked to my insurance company. I think it's rotten that they're only giving you a hundred and fifty dollars. I'm really sorry, Meg."

She waved it away. "They were right. That piece of junk was only worth a hundred and fifty."

"This is all my fault," he said, setting the heated dinner in front of her. "I'll make it up to you."

She nibbled at the turkey. "Yum. Maybe I wasn't depressed. Maybe I was just hungry. I'm feeling lots better. Any more dressing? Did you bring gravy?"

"Shoot, for a minute there I thought I had to marry you to get you cheered up, but hell, all I had to do was feed you."

"Hmmm. So, you're thinking about marrying me?"

"Actually, I'm thinking about thinking about marrying you. I'm working my way up to it."

"Gee whiz, how exciting. Do you have dessert in your bag?"

He produced an entire pumpkin pie. "It's scary, Meg. All those years in school, and then internship. I never thought past graduation. Now all of a sudden I'm a doctor, and I'm sort of bowled over by it."

"I understand," she said, slicing herself a

wedge of pie. "I really do. I've spent the better part of the afternoon sitting on a step, trying to get a grip on things and not succeeding. I thought I was sure, but now I don't know. Do you think indecision is catching?"

"Definitely. I had an entire course on it in pre-med. Indecision 101." He rinsed her empty plate and put it in the dishwasher. "I'd better get going. I have to be at the hospital early tomorrow, and it's a long walk home."

"You walked here?"

"Tomorrow I get my car. It wasn't badly damaged. They hammered out the fender and fixed the radiator."

"Lucky duck."

He kissed her lightly on the lips. "Hang in there," he said, hating himself for saying it. It was a feeble cliché. He'd smashed her car, ruined her weekend, and told her he was thinking about thinking about marrying her. And she'd been nice to him, thanking him for the food and understanding his panic. Hunter, he told himself, you're a crumb.

Megan burrowed under her pillow. She was having hallucinations. It was the middle of the night, and she could have sworn she'd heard Pat making a racket at her front door. That was ridiculous. Timmy was gone. Pat had no car. There was no explanation for the noise in her front yard.

She dragged herself out of bed and squinted into the predawn blackness. There was a taxi idling in her driveway, and yes, the lunatic doctor was at her front door. Now what? His house had burned down? Extraterrestrials were invading Tarplay's Store? She felt a smile creep through her body. It was nice to see him at her doorstep, no matter what the reason.

"Something wrong?" she asked, opening the door.

Pat stepped inside and groaned. Her mussed hair fell over her shoulders, forming a glowing frame around a face still soft with sleep. Her shoulders were bare and waiting to be kissed. One thin strap of her peach-colored satin nightie slid down her arm in erotic invitation. The gown was short, barely covering her bottom, leaving him to wonder if her outfit included panties. He'd intended to do a good deed, but it was a mistake. He could see that now. The memory of this nightie was going to keep him in a state of constant arousal. He'd have to wear a smock all day.

"Megan," he said. His voice sounded an octave higher than usual to his ears, so he cleared his throat and started again. "I can't stay. I'm on my way to the hospital. I just wanted to drop off some breakfast." He hefted several grocery bags from the front porch and placed them at her feet. A mischievous look came into his eyes. "About this sultry little number you're wearing . . ."

"Mmmm?" she purred.

His voice grew conspiratorially low. "Does it have . . . I mean, are you wearing . . ."

She smiled. "That's privileged information."

"Remember what you told me about a man's finding out things for himself?"

"Mmmm." Another purr.

He took a step toward her, and she retreated. When she spoke her voice was husky and hinting of laughter. "I can't help feeling cuddly about you, but that doesn't mean I'm going to allow liberties."

Pat thought he could go on looking at her forever. He loved seeing her laughing and rumpled from sleep. For two cents he'd tell the taxi to take a hike. Unfortunately, there were babies waiting for him at the hospital. He'd stayed longer than he should. He sighed heavily. "I don't have time for liberties anyway. Darn."

Megan deliberately yawned and stretched, lifting her arms above her head and raising the hem of her nightie high enough to elicit a another groan from Pat. "Thanks," she said. "It was nice of you to think of breakfast."

Pat staggered into the cold air and firmly closed the door behind him. He leaned against it for a moment to take a deep breath. He was being tortured. He was still paying the price for sending Dave home on a doughnut. Fate was getting even with him.

Megan carted a bag into the kitchen and unpacked it, thinking about how cute Pat had looked standing there in his crisp white shirt and red striped tie under his leather jacket and red scarf. His hair had been falling boyishly across his forehead in unkempt bangs.

He must be a real heart-breaker at the hospital, she thought. All the nurses were probably in love with him. Well, she had some advice for those nurses. Don't get your hopes up, girls. The man is not the marrying type. The man is strictly the love-'em-and-leave-'em type.

She lifted a carton of orange juice from the bag and reconsidered. Not exactly love 'em and leave 'em, she decided. More like love 'em and let 'em dangle. She wanted to be mad at him, but she couldn't. He couldn't help the way he felt, and he was being honest with her.

She put a half gallon of milk in the refrigerator and sighed. When she was done unpacking the groceries she was going back to bed. She was suddenly so tired, she could hardly breathe. There was a sadness inside her, so all-encompassing and overwhelming, it left her weak. It was enervating to have been surrounded by so much love and activity and then to have it suddenly stripped away.

Several hours later she once again dragged herself out of bed to stare out her window. Now what? It sounded like more cars in her driveway. She hadn't had this much company since her neighbor, old Mrs. Wipple, had mistaken the plume of black smoke spewing from Megan's tail pipe for a barn fire and phoned a false alarm in to the fire department.

A young man saw Megan at the window and waved. "Just delivering your new car, ma'am."

"I don't have a new car."

"You do now," he said, smiling. "I'll leave the keys in the glove compartment."

She pulled on jeans and a sweat shirt, hopped into a pair of boots, and ran downstairs. She threw open the front door and gaped at the shiny red car sitting in her driveway. It was one of those little Japanese cars, brand new, with a big white bow stuck to its door handle. A card had been taped to the window. It said: "Meg, sorry I smashed your car. Pat."

"Oh, hell." He was being nice again.

At one-thirty Megan called Pat.

A familiar male voice answered the phone. "Dr. Hunter's office. Dr. Hunter speaking."

"Pat? What on earth are you doing answering your own phone?"

"Megan? Did you get the car?"

"Yes. It's a great car, but—"

"It gets thirty miles to the gallon and has intermittent windshield wipers."

"I know, but—"

"It has front-wheel drive and radials."

"But—"

"Is red okay?"

"Pat! I can't keep this car!"

"Why not?"

"For one thing, how are you paying for it? I know you can't afford car payments." A thought flashed through her mind. "Patrick Hunter, where's your receptionist?"

"Listen, Megan, I'd love to chat, but this is runny-nose season, and I have a waiting room filled with sniffling kids."

"I don't want to be obligated to you for this car."

"You're not obligated. I was the one obligated. I wrecked your car, and I felt obligated to replace it. Besides, it's easier for me this way. I'm not constantly worrying about your driving that old maroon piece of junk."

"You worried about me?"

There was a moment of silence, and when Pat spoke it was in a low, intimate voice. "Of course I worried about you. I care about you."

She sighed. "In fact, you care about me

so much that you're thinking about thinking about marrying me?"

"Yes."

"Well, don't do me any favors," she said and hung up.

Chapter 11

On a Sunday afternoon Megan was perched on a high stool inside the wigmaker's shop, and peering out at a quickly darkening Williamsburg. When the weather was cooperative she checked tickets outdoors, standing just to the side of the shop entrance, but today the temperature had plummeted, forcing her to move indoors.

The sky was lead gray, and a few snowflakes drifted past the window. Candles had been lit to dispel the gloom in the shop, but their cozy glow did little to brighten Megan's mood. She hadn't seen Pat or spoken to him in six days. It seemed like six years.

Snow swirled against the glass panes and dusted the porch railing, isolating Megan from the rest of the world. Sounds were muffled, and visibility was limited to a few feet. Under other circumstances this would have been a time for her to play, but she didn't feel playful that day. She was relieved when it was five o'clock, and she could go home before road conditions became dangerous.

She said good-bye to the wigmaker and wrapped her black woolen cape tightly around herself, pulling the hood over her head. She'd parked in the lot on Francis Street, just a short distance away, but she was chilled to the bone by the time she reached her car.

Snow clung to her eyebrows and melted off the tip of her nose. She stamped her shoes and attempted to shake the snow from her cape before sliding behind the wheel.

The little red car purred to life, and for the first time in six days she was truly thankful Pat had insisted she keep the car. They'd agreed it would be a loan. He had reduced his receptionist's hours until after Christmas, when, Megan hoped, she would make enough money from her pottery to take over the car payments.

She slowly drove through the back streets, observing the newly hung eighteenth-century Christmas decorations. Red velvet bows and evergreen sprays adorned many of the private residences. Traditional Williamsburg wreaths of laurel, trimmed with fresh apples, pineapples, pine cones, and peanuts hung on doors. By next week the town would be alive with the spirit of Christmas, bracing itself for the onslaught of holiday tourists. Megan didn't want to think about it. Christmas was a family time, and she no longer had a family. She had a mother and father, of course, but they were far away.

She grimly stared at the back-street houses and wondered what activity was taking place behind the wreaths and bows. Windows glowed golden through the curtain of snow, and smoke curled from old brick chimneys. It was easy to imagine the laughter of children as they hunted for boots and scarves and begged their parents to get sleds down from summer hiding places in the garage.

She purposely avoided passing by Pat's house and Tilly Coogan's apartment. She couldn't bear the thought of being on the outside, looking in. She couldn't bear the pain of not belonging.

She carefully traveled the country road, becoming more tense as the snow deepened, grateful for the new tires and front-wheel drive, which held the car on the slick surface. She briefly closed her eyes in silent thanks when her driveway appeared. Be it ever so lonely, she thought, it was still good to be home.

She locked the car and went straight to the barn, cautiously opening the paddock door for the horse. When she'd first moved to the farm she'd tried to make friends with the animal, but it had been aloof, disdaining her clucking noises and ignoring offered apples. When its owner had appeared recently on Megan's doorstep at seven one Saturday morning, looking for a weekend horse sitter, Megan had jumped at the chance.

It wasn't the prettiest horse she had ever seen, nor the most charismatic, but it intrigued her all the same. And besides, she needed the money. Two scoops of grain, a slice of hay, and let it come inside for the night. Those were the instructions. Very simple.

It was a nice horse, Megan told herself as it obediently plodded toward its stall. It had soft brown eyes and a glossy black coat. It was just that horses were so big, and this particular horse seemed bigger than most, with a huge belly, large, clomping hooves, and enormous teeth. She gave it grain and hay and filled its water bucket with fresh water.

"Nice horse," she told it timidly, giving it a good-night pat on the forehead.

Once inside her house Megan retreated to the kitchen. She made herself a cup of hot chocolate and a ham sandwich and sat at the round wood table, sketching new designs and planning formulas for new glazes for her pots.

Outside the wind howled under the eaves, and snow pinged against frosted windowpanes. When a particularly ferocious gust of wind buffeted the old house, Megan looked up in surprise. It was eleven-thirty by the cuckoo clock on the kitchen wall.

The barn door blew open with a slam, and she scowled at the thought of going outdoors. She had to check on the horse, she reminded herself firmly. She had to make sure it was warm enough.

This was silly, she thought as she trudged through the snow. She wouldn't know a cold horse if she saw one, and if it was cold, she wouldn't know what to do about it. She switched the barn lights on and was greeted by a low whinny that caused all the little hairs to stand up on her neck.

The horse was moving about its large box stall, restless and agitated. It rolled its eyes at Megan, showing the whites, and gave another whinny from deep in its throat. Its belly bulged awkwardly hanging heavy.

"Holy smoke," Megan whispered. The horse looked deranged. Probably from carrying that bloated stomach around. It looked as if it had eaten a small cow.

"Listen," she said to the horse, "don't worry about it. I'll get a vet. He'll know what to do. Probably you just need some Pepto Bismol. About two gallons of it."

She copied the vet's number from the barn wall, ran back to the kitchen, dialed the number, and waited. No answer. Great. The horse was dying at eleven-thirty on a Sunday night in the middle of a raging blizzard. Her chances of finding a vet were about as good as her chances of flying to Tokyo without a plane.

Stay calm, she told herself. If you can't get a vet, then call a doctor! That was insane. What doctor would come out on a night like this to look at a hyper horse? Pat.

Half an hour later Pat slowly drove his car into a ditch at the entrance to Megan's driveway. He crawled through the passenger side window, catapulted himself off the tilted chassis into a waist-high snowbank, and quickly ran through his entire repertoire of expletives.

He was wading through the storm of the century, in the middle of the night, to examine a horse. He'd have liked to think it was a ruse Megan had constructed to bring them together, but he knew better. Not even Megan could think up something as dumb as this. A horse, for crying out loud. He didn't know anything about horses.

He'd been in a black mood for six days, and slogging through knee-high snow wasn't doing much to improve his disposition. He missed Megan, dammit. He missed her every second of every minute of every day. And he was furious with himself for missing her. He should have known better than to fall in love with a stubborn redhead. When Megan did something, she did it all the way. A hundred and three percent. She was ... overwhelming.

He opened the barn door, and was happy

for the warmth he found there. Megan had dragged her space heater into the building. She'd also draped a full-size feather quilt over the obese horse and tied it on with baling twine. She was standing beside the stall, wringing her hands, and he smiled in spite of himself. She was singing nursery rhymes, trying to calm the crazy horse.

"Looks like you're taking good care of my patient," he said softly.

She whirled around to face him. "I don't know what to do for it!" she cried. "I tried calling the owner and the vet but no one answered. I don't know anything about horses."

Pat looked at the horse. It seemed bigger than he'd remembered.

"So what's wrong with it? Measles? Sore throat? Diaper rash? I hope it's one of those, Megan. They're my specialty."

"Um, no. It's none of those. It's just acting weird."

"You called me over here because the horse is acting weird?"

"I think it ate something awful. Its stomach is all distended."

Pat cautiously approached the horse and

untied the baling twine. "Nice horsey," he said, sliding the quilt off. "Nice *fat* horsey. Looks like it ate a car."

Suddenly the horse's knees buckled and the animal rolled onto its side.

"Holy cow!" Pat said, jumping back. He cleared his throat and blushed. "Took me by surprise."

"Oh, Pat, what's wrong with it? I don't know much about horses, but I know they're supposed to be standing up. It's not going to die, is it?"

He knelt beside the animal and ran his hand along the straining belly. "Honey, I'm afraid you called the wrong doctor. This horse doesn't need a pediatrician. It needs an obstetrician."

"You mean it's having a baby? Can it do it by itself?"

"Lord, I hope so."

After ten minutes Pat felt the mare's belly again and shook his head. "I don't know much about this, but I don't think she's progressing the way she should. Keep her calm. I'll be right back."

Within minutes he'd returned, carrying a sheet and a plastic bag. "Let's get the sheet under her as best we can. Tie her tail up in the plastic bag so it's out of my way."

He took off his jacket, sweater, and shirt and knelt behind the horse. "I'm scrubbed up to my armpits. Let's hope once I get my hand in there, I can get it back out!"

"Good heavens, you mean you're going to . . . um, examine her?"

"This would be a good time to sing one of those nursery rhymes. I'd rather she wasn't thinking about what I'm doing down here."

"Okay, horse," Megan said cheerfully. "We're all going to work together to have a baby now. Are you listening?"

"It's the legs," Pat said. "I don't think she can deliver in this position. I can see a nose and a hoof, but the second leg is stuck. I have to ease it up beside the first one."

The horse was grunting like mad, and Megan was nervous. "Are you sure you can do that?" she asked.

"Megan, I've delivered a bunch of human babies, a litter of kittens when I was ten, and I've read *All Things Great and Small*. That's the extent of my veterinary knowledge. I'm not sure of anything, but I'm going to try."

A minute later he sat back on his heels and grinned. "I did it! A few good contractions, and it should slide right out."

Minutes later the wobbly newborn was standing next to its mother, who licked at its wet body.

Megan's cheeks were soaked with tears. "It's a miracle," she said with a gasp, choked with emotion. "I've never seen a birth. I've never seen anything so beautiful."

Pat examined the mare, and pronounced her sound. Then he collapsed against the side of the stall to watch his newest patient.

"Tired?" Megan asked.

"Naw, not me. That was a piece of cake. You have any other animals you want me to deliver? A cow? Maybe an elephant?"

She sat beside him, her face glowing with love and pride. "You were wonderful."

"You were, too. I couldn't have done it without you."

"We're a team."

His gaze held hers. They were a team, he thought. In every sense of the word. And he couldn't for the life of him imagine why the thought of marriage had frightened him.

The foal stood on spindly legs and nuzzled at its mother's belly, searching for its first meal. It took a step forward and stumbled. It righted itself, wagged its tail, and succeeded in its search.

"It's a beautiful baby," Megan said proudly.

Pat grinned. He'd heard that tone of voice before, and he strongly suspected Megan would want to adopt the horse. Well, hell, if that was what she wanted . . . How hard could it be to adopt a horse? Probably they should get legally married first. Wouldn't want an illegitimate horse, he thought, feeling lighthearted and foolish.

He wanted to reach out to Megan, to untie her braids and snuggle next to her in the hay, but he needed to get clean first. "I'm afraid I'm not such a neat obstetrician," he said, ineffectually wiping his hands on a towel. "Can I use your shower?"

Megan swallowed. Patrick Hunter in her shower. Naked. What a lovely thought. If she played her cards right, she could probably get him into her bed. What the heck? she thought. He was already firmly implanted in her heart.

Yup, she was ready to dangle, to hang in

there, to fight for her man. No more pouting over hurt feelings and old insecurities. She was going to convince Pat that marriage would be wonderful. Any man who could deliver a horse could live through marriage, she decided.

"Of course you can use my shower. You go ahead, and I'll close up the barn."

She shoveled out the soiled bedding and spread a clean layer of fresh sawdust over the stall floor. She left the lights on, knowing they'd be checking on the horses throughout the night, closed the barn door, secured the latch, and winced as wind-driven snow pelted her face and stung her eyes.

She found Pat sitting in her bed, sipping brandy, covers precariously draped across his bare hips. His hair was damp from his shower, and his smile reminded her of the Big Bad Wolf.

"I didn't have a thing to wear," he explained.

"Hmmm," she said, stealing a taste of brandy. "There's always my bathrobe."

"No way. Last time I wore your bathrobe I got punched in the nose."

She eased onto the bed and leaned over him.

"It's such a cute nose, too," she said and kissed the tip of it.

He loosened a braid. "Was that a pretend kiss?"

"Nope. No more pretending."

"So, this is the real thing now, huh?" he asked, looking very serious.

"Yup."

He pulled her onto his lap. "Good. I love the real thing." His gaze softened. "And I love you."

Megan felt the breath catch in her throat. "What?"

"I love you," he said, feeling like the Grinch, whose heart had grown three sizes on Christmas Day.

She gave a huge sigh of satisfaction. "I love you too."

"Now that we love each other, I suppose it would be okay if I spent the night here."

"It'll cost ya," she said.

His breathing grew heavy as he stared at her mouth. It was a lovely pink rosebud mouth. Soft and kissable. "What's the price?"

She suggestively whispered an erotic payment. Then she licked her lips and mentioned an alternative, feeling smugly satisfied at the hint of movement under the blanket.

"Megan Murphy, shame on you. That's very naughty."

She turned the cover back. "Don't you want to pay my price?" she asked, all innocence.

"I suppose I'll have to, but only if you'll marry me. I have my reputation to think of. I have morals and principles."

"I wouldn't want to besmirch your reputation. And I certainly wouldn't want to trample on your morals and principles."

He unbuttoned her flannel shirt. "In case you're wondering, that was a proposal. A very serious, very binding proposal."

She drew back and looked at him. "Are you sure?"

"I've never been more sure of anything in my entire life."

"Would a Christmas wedding be too soon?"

"A Christmas wedding would be too late. I intend to consummate this union immediately. And now, Megan Murphy-Hunter, I'm going to follow your erotically imaginative suggestions and deliver payment in full!"

If you loved
Thanksgiving
check out this sneak peek from
Smitten
by Janet Evanovich

available now from HarperTorch

When Lizabeth Kane was five years old she wanted to grow up to be a fairy. She wanted skin that was as smooth and white as milkweed silk. And she wanted hair that cascaded halfway down her back in a luxuriant cloud of waves and curls that shone a sunny yellow by day and silver when washed by the light of the moon. She thought she'd wear a buttercup blossom when she needed a hat, and she'd go rafting on curled magnolia leaves.

At five Lizabeth understood that she was a human child and it would take some doing to shrink herself into fairy size, but she had confidence in falling stars and wishbones and birthday candles. She knew that fairies were tiny creatures, no bigger than a man's thumb, but it seemed to her that if a girl could grow up, then she could almost as easily grow down. And if she could eventually grow breasts, then probably if she tried very hard she could grow wings instead. Almost all fairies had lovely gossamer wings, and Lizabeth wasn't sure how comfortable that would be when she wanted to sleep on her back or lean against the gnarled trunk of an enchanted tree to daydream. She supposed that would be part of the price she would pay for growing up to be a fairy.

In fact, that was about the only price exacted on an adult fairy, because for the most part, fairies did just as they pleased. They weren't stuffed into panty hose and sent off on a bus to earn a living staring at a computer screen. They weren't polite to incompetent employers for the sake of career advancement. And they weren't expected to prepare gourmet feasts for boring men who had only one thing on their minds . . . lasagna.

Fairies were indulgent, playful creatures, and even though two decades and several years had gone by since Lizabeth first decided to be a fairy, even though Lizabeth Kane now stood five feet six inches tall in her stocking feet, even though she was thirty-two years old—she still had aspirations of growing up to be a fairy.

She no longer cared about whittling herself down to the average fairy height of five inches, or having milkweed skin or gobs of fairy hair. Lizabeth Kane wanted the pluck, the joie de vivre, the perfect thighs of Tinkerbell. Think positive, Lizabeth told herself. If she just put her mind to it she could be plucky, she could have joie de vivre—and two out of three wasn't bad.

She folded the morning paper under her arm and looked at the half-finished house looming in front of her. She had to be positive about getting a job, too. She was a single parent now, and if she didn't get a job soon, meeting her mortgage payment was going to be more elusive than obtaining Tinkerbell thighs.

She read the crude HELP WANTED sign stuck into the front yard and took a deep breath. She'd been on fourteen job interviews in the past five days, and no one had even given her a second look. She was overeducated. She was undereducated. She was inexperienced. She was unskilled. She was virtually unemployable. Okay, Lizabeth, she said to herself, pulling her shoulders back, this is a new day. This is your last shot. And this is the perfect job. Perfect hours, perfect location, decent wages. Go for it! she told herself.

Matt Hallahan had been looking out an upstairs window. He'd watched Lizabeth fold her paper and chew on her lower lip while she stared at the house. Not a buyer, he decided. Buyers came in pairs and usually had a real-estate agent in tow. This woman looked as if she were peddling vacuum cleaners and he was her first customer. She was nervous, she was anxious—she was cute as a bug. Even from this distance he could see she had big blue eyes, a little nose, and lots of curly brown hair that hung almost to her shoulders. She was small-boned and slim. Not skinny. Her pink T-shirt stretched tight over full breasts and was tucked into a pair of formfitting, faded jeans. He didn't know what she was selling, but he admitted to himself that he'd have a hard time not buying it.

Outside, Lizabeth stiffened her spine, pushed her chin forward, and tiptoed through the mud to the front door.

"Yoo-hoo," she called. "Anybody home?"

She gasped and took a step backward when Matt appeared at the head of the stairs and ambled down to her. He was big. He seemed to fill the whole stairwell. He was half-undressed, and he was gorgeous.

She felt her heart slam against the back of her rib cage while she made a fast assessment. At least six feet two inches, with broad shoulders and a flat stomach and slim hips. No shirt, jeans that rode low, a red heart tattooed on his left forearm. He had muscular legs. Great quads. And he was tan—everywhere.

When she finally dragged her eyes up to his face she found he was laughing at her. Smile lines splintered from deep-set blue eyes that were shaded by curly blond eyelashes and a ferocious slash of bushy blond eyebrows. His nose was sunburned and peeling.

"Lord, lady," he said, "last time someone looked at me that close was when I thought I had a hernia and the doctor told me to cough."

Lizabeth felt the flush spread from her ears to her cheeks. Get a grip, she told herself. Thirty-two-year-old mothers do not blush. She'd delivered two children, she'd learned to pump gas, she'd seen Tom Cruise and Cuba Gooding Jr. on screen in their underwear. She could handle anything. She ignored his remark and plastered a smile on her face.

"I'd like to speak to whoever is in charge of this construction project."

"That's me. Matt Hallahan." He held out his hand.

"Lizabeth Kane." He didn't rub his thumb across her wrist. He didn't give her an extra squeeze or prolong the contact. He just shook her hand. She liked him for that. And she liked the way his hand felt. Warm and calloused and firm.

"I'd like to apply for the job you advertised in the paper."

Matt missed a beat before answering. "I advertised for a carpenter."

"Yup."

His grin widened. Life was full of nice surprises. "You have any experience?"

"Actually, I haven't done much carpentering professionally. But I've hammered a lot of nails into things—you know, hanging pictures—and once I built a dollhouse from scratch, all by myself."

The smile tightened at the corners of his mouth. "That's it?"

"I suppose I was hoping it would be an entry-level position."

"Entry level in the construction business would be laborer."

Lizabeth caught her bottom lip between her teeth. "Oh. Well then, I'd like to apply for a job as a laborer."

"Honey, you're too little to be a laborer. Laborers do a lot of carting around." He squeezed her biceps. "Look at this. Hardly any muscle at all. You probably have one of those motor-driven Hoovers."

Lizabeth narrowed her eyes. She didn't like being called a wimp. "I can do a push-up."

"Only one?"

"One is pretty good. Besides, I've just started on my exercise program. Next week I'll be up to two . . . maybe three."

"Wouldn't you rather be a secretary? You could work in a nice air-conditioned office . . ."

"No," Lizabeth said firmly. "I would not rather be a secretary. To begin with, I can't type. I break out in hives when I sit in front of a computer screen. I can't do *anything*! You know why I can't do anything? Because when I went to college I majored in history. My mother told me to major in math, but did I listen to her? Nooooo. I could have been an accountant. I could have been self-employed. And if that isn't bad enough, I've spent the last ten years of my life reading Little Bear books and baking chocolate-chip cookies."

She was pacing, flapping her arms. "Now I need a job, and I can't do anything. If I don't get a job, I can't meet my mortgage payments. My kids will starve. I heard of a woman once who got so desperate she cooked her dog." Lizabeth gave an involuntary shiver.

"You have kids?"

"Two boys. Ten and eight. You see, that's why this job is so perfect for me. I only live about a quarter mile away. I've been watching the new houses going up, and I noticed the carpenters stop work at three-thirty. My kids get out of school at three-thirty. I wouldn't have to put them in day care if I worked here."

He looked at her left hand. No ring. He was doomed. How could he refuse a job to a woman who was about to barbecue Spot to keep her kids from starving?

"I'm much bigger than I look," Lizabeth said. "And besides, that's another thing about the job that's perfect. It would get me into shape. And I would learn things about a house. I need to know about fixing toilets and roofs and getting tiles to stick to floors."

"How soon do you have to know all these things?"

"The sooner the better."

Matt grimaced. "Your roof is leaking? Your toilet has a problem? Your tiles are coming loose?"

"Yes. But it's not as bad as it sounds. I bought this terrific house. It was built at the turn of the century and has gingerbread trim and elaborate cornices and wonderful woodwork, but it's a little run-down . . ."

"You're not talking about that gray Victorian on the corner of Woodward and Gainsborough, are you?"

Lizabeth nodded. "That's it. That's my house."

"I always thought that house was haunted. In fact, I thought it was condemned."

"It's not haunted. And it was only condemned because the front porch needed fixing."

She paused in her pacing and looked at him. "You don't think it's hopeless, do you?"

He wasn't sure if she was talking about her house or his life after this moment. It didn't matter. The answer would be the same to both questions—yes. But he lied. "No. I think the house has . . . possibilities. It has . . . character."

Lizabeth smiled. She loved her house. It had a few problems, but it was charming and homey and just looking at it made her happy. She'd bought it in January, the day after her divorce had become final. She'd needed to do something positive. Give herself a symbolic fresh start.

"Maybe you could come over sometime and take a look at it. You could give me your professional opinion on it. I'm not sure which project I should start first."

His professional opinion was that the house should be burned to the ground. He wasn't able to tell her that, though, because his heart was painfully stuck in his throat. It had happened when she'd smiled. She had the most beautiful, the most radiant smile he'd ever seen. And he'd caused it just by saying her house had character.

Lizabeth saw his eyes grow soft and sexy and worried that he'd misinterpreted her invitation. She hadn't meant to be so friendly. She didn't want to imply that she'd do *anything* to get the job. It was just that it was difficult for her to be less than exuberant when it came to her house. And in all honesty, she might have gaped at his body a tad too long.

"I didn't mean to sound so desperate for the job," she said. "This is my first construction interview, and I think I got carried away. I don't want you to hire me because you feel sorry for me with my leaky roof and two hungry kids. And I don't want you to hire me because . . . well, you know."

He raised his eyebrows in question.

Lizabeth was disgusted. She was making a fool of herself. She'd approached him about a job and had ended up telling him her life story, and now she was in the awkward position of establishing sexual boundaries. She'd been separated from her husband for a year and a half and divorced for six months, but she still wasn't especially good at being a sophisticated single. It wasn't a matter of time, she admitted. It was a matter of personality. She was an impulsive, let-it-all-hang-out, emotional dunderhead.

"Look," she said flatly, "I'm willing to work hard. I'm smart. I'm dependable. I'm honest."

She pulled a folded piece of lined notebook paper from her pocket and handed it to him. "This is my résumé. It's not much, but it has my name and address and phone number, and if you ever need a laborer, you can get in touch with me."

Matt unfolded the paper and studied it, trying to keep the grin from creeping across his mouth. "This is a spelling list."

Lizabeth snatched it back and winced as she looked at it. "I took the wrong paper. This is my son's homework assignment."

"Don't worry about it. I don't need a résumé. And it so happens I do need a laborer."

"You're not hiring me out of pity, are you?"

"No, of course not." That was an honest answer, he thought. He was hiring her out of lust. He didn't think she wanted to hear that, so he decided not to elaborate. "You can start tomorrow, if you want. Be here at six o'clock."

She did it! She got the job! If Matt Hallahan hadn't been so overwhelmingly virile, she would have kissed him, but she instinctively knew kissing Matt Hallahan would be serious stuff. It would start out as a spontaneous act of happiness and gratitude, and it would end up as pure pleasure. A fairy wouldn't have hesitated for a second, but Lizabeth Kane wasn't a fairy. She was a mother, so she gave herself a mental hug and smiled.

Matt couldn't help smiling back. Her joy was infectious. He stuffed his hands into his pockets, and wondered what the devil he was going to do with a soft, gullible, 125-pound laborer.

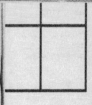